"Why Don'[...]
And Leave Me Alone?"

She spun away from him. "You're not my keeper. Go back and save someone else's life."

Gently but firmly, he grasped her by the upper arm, stopping her in her tracks. "The way you've been pushing yourself you need a keeper." His voice had a ragged edge. Turning to face her, he clasped her other arm. "It might as well be me."

"I don't think so," Becca retorted, a shiver rippling through her when he raised his hand to cradle her face. "You're the last person..."

"Be quiet for once." With that he very effectively shut her up himself, by covering her mouth with his.

Dear Reader,

Hello, dear friend, I hope this finds you well and happy.

The M.D.'s Mistress is the first in the four-book series, GIFTS FROM A BILLIONAIRE. All four stories center around a mysterious billionaire who gives four unsuspecting heroines a monetary gift destined to change their lives…and bring them unexpected love.

I hope you will enjoy all of the stories, written by myself and three of my very good friends and fellow authors: Leslie LaFoy, a terrific writer of historical and contemporary stories; Mary McBride, another writer with a large following; and Kasey Michaels, a writer known for her contemporary, historical and mystery stories. This talented lady happens to be one of my very best friends... in addition to being very funny.

So, there you have it, gentle reader. I sincerely hope you enjoy all four books…starting with the one you are now holding in your hands.

My best always,

Joan Hohl

JOAN HOHL

THE M.D.'S MISTRESS

Published by Silhouette Books
America's Publisher of Contemporary Romance

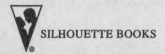

SILHOUETTE BOOKS

ISBN-13: 978-0-373-76892-9
ISBN-10:   0-373-76892-3

THE M.D.'S MISTRESS

JOAN HOHL

is a *New York Times* bestselling author. She has received numerous awards for her work, including a Romance Writers of America Golden Medallion Award. Joan lives in eastern Pennsylvania with her husband and family.

To the gang: Kathie, Marcie, Leslie and Mary.

Thank you all for being my friends. Life would be duller without the four of you wacky ladies! Love you all.

Prologue

And to wrap up our first column of the New Year, darlings, that delicious rumor has bubbled to the surface yet again. Remember the one about the reclusive billionaire who anonymously surprises the worthy with tax-free million-dollar checks each Christmas season? Well, boys and girls, it would seem that last year was no exception.

Or so we hear.

This time, however, our rumor's got a new twist.

Supposedly, our RB—that's Reclusive Billionaire, darlings—actually starts small, sending anonymous gifts throughout the year to each of those who have impressed him in some way, then sits back to watch what happens next.

Continue to make Santa happy, and maybe there's a cool million in your Christmas stocking. Do those who don't continue to live up to RB's unknown standards get a sack of coal? Or perhaps just a note saying, "Sorry, maybe next time you'll be nice, not naughty." Details! We need details!

Who knows exactly how this generous Santa operates? After all, this is only the latest whisper on the same rumor that's been tickling our fancy for years. Your favorite columnist, who would be *moi,* is still on the story but, so far, all of Santa's helpers have been mum.

In the meantime, you read it here first. It could be fiscally sound to be nice this year, darlings!

The clipping was muttered over, then dropped to the already crowded desktop.

"Yes, I saw that one, too, Uncle Ned," said the man sitting at ease on the other side of his wide teak desk. "We see a handful of stories in one form or another after every holiday season. Are you worried? Do you want to discontinue the program?"

His answer was a frown that would have most other men ducking for cover under the closest chair.

This man merely smiled, and shook his head. "No, I didn't think so. You're such an old softie, *Santa*."

One

It was raining. Again. It wasn't a downpour, but a gentle rain, wet just the same, and chilly.

Becca, shoulders hunched with exhaustion, trudged back to her lodging, such as it was in the tiny African village that everyone, including God, seemed to have forgotten.

After over eighteen months in the village, Becca was beyond weary. There were times when she wasn't sure she could keep going, but the people needed her as much as the small hospital, which had been built by the generosity of American philanthropists. And she had come to love the people, especially the children, with their sweet faces and innocent dark eyes.

Rebecca Jameson had been an O.R. nurse at the University of Pennsylvania Hospital for several years before volunteering to go serve in this small hospital in Africa. Working ten, twelve and sometimes as many as fourteen hours a day, every day, was beginning to wear on her.

Becca knew she should heed the advice of just about everyone urging her to accept a replacement and go back to the States for a long rest. But since Dr. Seth Andrews, the very talented but equally arrogant surgeon, had all but demanded she go, she stubbornly refused to leave.

Grateful for about the hundredth time for being advised to bring boots with her, Becca slogged along the squishy ground, her mind replaying the long shift she had moments ago completed. She sighed. For some reason Dr. I'm-The-Boss-And-You're-Not Andrews had been exceptionally cranky throughout the entire day.

Head lowered, concentrating on putting one foot in front of the other, Becca frowned as her sight became gray, darker than the overcast sky. What—

It was her last thought as darkness closed in, enveloping her. The next moment, she toppled over onto her face, out cold....

Becca surfaced slowly from unconsciousness.

Her head ached. Her entire body hurt. Her mind felt fuzzy, as if it were stuffed with cotton.

Her first thought wasn't, *where am I?* It was, *pain, so much pain.* She made a soft moan of protest.

"Oh, finally awake are you? I told you that you were exhausted."

Even with her mind cloudy, Becca recognized the barely civil voice of Dr. Andrews. "I guess so," she replied, her voice an unfamiliar croak. "So, I suppose I'll live to irritate you another day." She decided her brain must have been rattled, or she'd have never had the nerve to speak to the Great One that way.

"No, you won't, smart mouth." His tone was menacing.

"I'm going to die?"

"No, Rebecca, you're not going to die." Now his tone carried a note of amusement. "You're going home."

Home? *No!* The word rang loud and clear inside her muddled head. Despite his obvious dislike of her, and his equally obvious desire to get rid of her, Becca didn't want to leave. She just couldn't leave the children. And, secretly, she didn't want to leave him, and not see him again, either.

Besides, as grumpy as he was, Seth Andrews was the very best physician and surgeon she had ever worked with, in and out of the O.R.

"I...don't...want..." she began, her throat tight with anxiety.

"I don't care what you want," he said, his voice flat and adamant. "You are worn-out. The next time you'd go down..." He paused, drew a sharp breath. "Well, there's not going to be a next time. I've called for transport. You're going stateside, like it or not."

"But..." she tried to protest.

"No *buts,* Rebecca. You're going home. Period. Now, shut up while I examine you."

Becca closed her eyes to hold back the tears welling behind them. Damn him. She flinched slightly at the cold feel of the stethoscope on her bare flesh.

Her bare flesh.

A sudden, unwanted tingle slid the length of her body at the realization of her breasts being bared to him. He's a physician, for pity's sake, she reminded herself, gritting her teeth to contain the sensation. She sighed with a mixture of relief and disappointment when she felt her gown once again covering her.

"You're a little congested." He frowned. "Still, you're good to go."

Her eyes popped open. "Can I get up?" She stared at him. He appeared exhausted, strained. Lines of weariness scored his thin, chiseled face. If anything, he looked worse than he had the last time she had seen him. When was that, she wondered... yesterday, maybe?

"No." He shook his head, setting his too long thatch of dark hair in motion.

Becca had always thought he had beautiful, shiny hair. But now, he badly needed a decent haircut. She wasn't about to tell him that. She wasn't up to his scalding rebuke.

She closed her eyes again.

"That's right. Sleep, you need it."

As if he didn't. Becca kept the thought to herself. His lack of rest was his problem.

She was out again in moments. This time she fell into a deep, normal sleep.

When Becca woke the second time, the headache was gone, or mostly gone, very likely from whatever medication he'd ordered running through her IV. Her body still hurt all over, but not as much as before.

"Feeling any better?"

Not his voice. With a sigh of relief, Becca opened her eyes, smiling at the pretty, coffee-colored face of the young nurse standing by her bed. "Yes," she answered, her voice still a dry croak. "I'm thirsty."

The nurse, Shakana, smiled back. "I'm not surprised. You've been asleep a long time." Her English was flawless, not only because she had attended an American university, but also because she had diligently practiced it…with Becca's help ever since she had come to Shakana's village.

Watching as the young woman filled a cup with water for her, Becca asked, "How long have I been here…I mean since I keeled over in the road?"

"You went down the day, or evening, before yesterday."

"Two days." Becca croaked, gratefully excepting a few sips of the cool water from the straw Shakana offered her. "I'm concussed?" It was obvious, of course she was concussed. She had done a header, hadn't she?

"Yes, a mild concussion." Shakana smiled. "How's the headache?"

"Better." She managed a faint smile. "But the memory lingers on."

"You were exhausted, Becca, or you wouldn't have collapsed. You simply couldn't go anymore."

Becca sighed, and blinked at the tears misting her eyes. "And now he's sending me home," she said, her voice still faint, but hard-edged with bitterness.

Grabbing a tissue from a box next to the bed, Shakana wiped away the tears running down Becca's face. "Don't cry," she said. "It's for the best."

"Best for who?" Becca cried in a croak. "For me or him?"

"Whom." Shakana smiled.

"Who, whom, what the hell difference does it make?" She was crying harder. "I don't want to go, and he knows it. I want to stay here, work with you…" She was now sobbing. "He doesn't like me, so he's using my fall as an excuse to get rid of me."

"Oh, Becca, no," Shakana said, still mopping away the tears. "You didn't fall, you collapsed. Dr. Andrews doesn't dislike you…" She hesitated, bit her lip. "I think. He is a physician, and he is right about your condition. You're worn-out."

"But I could rest here," Becca protested. "A couple days of rest and I could—"

"No, Becca, you couldn't," Shakana interrupted. "It won't be enough. Have you looked at yourself in a mirror lately?"

"Well, of course I have, every morn—"

Shakana again cut her off. "No, I don't mean a quick glance while brushing your teeth, or your hair. I mean really looked, stark naked."

Becca shook her head, wincing at the stab of pain. "No, why in the world would I do that?" she asked with sharp impatience.

"Why indeed?" the nurse drawled. "Gee, you don't know you're practically down to nothing but skin and bones, do you?"

"Oh, come on, Shak," Becca protested, using the nickname she had given her friend. "I know I've lost a little weight, but…" In truth, she was well aware she had lost a lot of weight, but still she felt compelled to deny it.

"A little weight?" Shakana repeated in astonishment. "Becca, you are skinny, hardly any flesh on your bones at all. Your clothes hang on you." She gave Becca a shrewd look. "Oh, I know you've been wearing smaller tops, but your scrub pants literally hang on your hips, and despite the elastic waistband, I think the only thing holding them up is your protruding hip bones."

Becca bit her lips, admitting, "I was going to get a smaller pair of pants, when I got around to it."

Crossing her arms over her ample breasts, Shakana gave her an arch look, murmuring, "Uh-huh."

Becca couldn't help a weak smile. "Well, I thought about getting a smaller pair."

Shakana shook her head, her dark eyes sad. "Oh, Becca, I'm going to miss you so much. But it's time for you to go home, rest, put on some weight. Dear friend, it hurts me to see you like this."

Tears welled in Becca's eyes. "Come with me, Shak, please."

Those sad dark eyes grew misty. "I can't, Becca. You know that. This is my home."

"I know." Becca heaved a deep sigh, coughing with what she thought was the emotional tightness in her chest. "I know," she repeated, accepting another tissue from her best friend.

Crying softly after Shakana had left to check on her many other patients, Becca fell into a deep dreamless sleep once more.

At the jostling of her body, Becca was startled awake. What…? she thought, her eyes opening wide as she realized she was being moved onto a litter.

Shakana was there, and Dr. Andrews, directing the procedure, of course.

"Shakana?" she croaked from her dry-as-dust throat. "Why am I being moved?"

"The plane is here for you," Dr. Andrews said, his voice devoid of inflection.

"But, my stuff…" she began.

Shakana squeezed her hand. "I packed your things for you, Becca."

"But…" Heaving a long sigh, Becca gave up, knowing protest was pointless. She glanced around at the men handling the litter. From their uniforms and insignia, she could tell they were an American rescue team.

"I'm so thirsty, can I have some water, please?" She looked to Shakana, but it was Dr. Andrews who moved, holding up his hand to halt the crew. Taking the cup Shakana handed him, he put the straw to Becca's lips. His fingers lightly brushed her chin. The light touch rippled through Becca like a minor earthquake.

Shaken by the odd sensation, she quickly gulped the cool water and moved her face away from his hand, settling her head on the pillow. "Thank you," she murmured, not daring to look at him.

"You're welcome." His voice was harsh with an angry tinge.

Confused by his tone, and the possible reason for it, Becca stole a glance at him. He had turned away, again motioning the men to go.

Before they started to roll the litter away, another man walked into her line of vision. Becca frowned in confusion, because the man was wearing scrubs and a white coat. Stopping beside her, he took her wrist into his hand to take her pulse.

Becca frowned.

He smiled. "I'm Dr. Devos. And your pulse is a little rapid."

"She's a little anxious and upset, Doctor," Shakana said. "She doesn't want to leave."

"It's best, Ms. Jameson." He smiled again. "If you'll excuse the expression, you look like hell."

Somewhere around forty, he looked so kind, his smile was so gentle, she had no choice but to smile back. "I'll excuse you…this time."

"I told you she was exhausted, Jim."

Becca shifted her gaze to Dr. Andrews. In her opinion, he looked worse than she felt. Apparently Dr. Devos agreed with her assessment.

"So are you, Seth. That's why I'm here to replace you."

"What?"

Becca was shifting her glance from one to the

other, her mind echoing Dr. Andrews's angry and sharply voiced question.

"You've been ordered home. You can take all the time you need to gather your things." He paused, grinned and added, "So long as you do it within the hour."

"Jim, this is ridiculous."

"Sorry, Seth, it's out of my hands." He turned to smile at Becca. "You may spend some time with your friend here—" he indicated Shakana with a nod of his head "—until Dr. Andrews is ready."

"Thank you, Doctor." Her voice was thick with gratitude. She was ill and had just met him, yet Becca already knew she liked this soft-voiced man. Besides, he had thrown Dr. Andrews a curveball! She smiled.

"You're welcome." Smiling back, he turned to the rescue squad. "Take the litter to one of the empty examining rooms, so the nurses can get this bed ready for another patient." From the men, he looked at Shakana. "You have permission to stay with your patient until Dr. Andrews is ready." With a smile to both women, he strode away.

Holding Becca's hand, Shakana walked beside the litter to the empty examining room. Tears welled in Becca's eyes as the rescue team closed the door behind them. Shakana was ready with a tissue to mop up the flow.

"Where did that nice Dr. Devos and the crew come from? The States?" She sniffed. "And how did they know Dr. Andrews needed a replacement, too?"

"The doctor and the crew came by military jet from the States, and the helicopter came from Israel." A self-satisfied smile shadowed her lips. "Dr. Andrews asked me to make the arrangements. I'm the one who told them he needed a break as badly as you."

Becca wanted to laugh. Instead she started crying all over again, which brought on a fit of coughing. "I'm sorry." She sniffed, accepting another tissue to blow her nose. "But…I feel so, so…"

"I know," Shakana said, her smile now soft, gentle. "I want to cry with you."

"You'd better not," Becca cautioned, trying to sniff and smile at the same time. "What would those guys on the team think, finding two blubbering women when they come for me?" She felt the tears well again, and impatiently swiped her hand over her cheeks. "I'm over it," she said, drawing a breath and sighing. "Resigned to going."

"It really is best for you, Becca. I can't tell you how very concerned I, as well as all the people in the village, have been about you."

"They've all noticed me slowing down, I suppose."

"No, you haven't slowed down, that's your problem," her friend answered. "We've all noticed you dwindling down, week after week."

Becca coughed again, on the tears clogging her throat, she figured. "I love them, Shak."

The other woman's smile was warm with affection. "I know. We all love you back."

Fortunately for Becca, she was saved from completely breaking down by the rescue team returning to collect her. She squeezed Shakana's hand, hard, as if afraid of letting go.

Shakana squeezed back. "I can't walk with you to the plane. I must get back to work." She hesitated, tears beginning to seep down her face. "Get well soon, Becca. I'll miss you."

"I'll miss you, too." Becca was crying again. "I'll be in touch online," she promised, reluctantly releasing her hand.

"You'd better." Shakana was openly crying now. "Goodbye, Becca." She stepped back to let the men move into place at the litter.

Miserable, hating Seth Andrews, she waved goodbye to the people crowded outside the hospital and along the road to the small airfield where a large rescue helicopter sat waiting. She never noticed the two photographers in the midst of the people, snapping away as she passed by.

Dr. Andrews was already in the chopper, looking angry and disgusted. Becca hoped he hadn't found out Shakana had been the one to turn him in...so to speak.

Within minutes, the experienced crew had settled her comfortably inside the craft. Not wanting to look at Seth's grim expression, she closed her eyes and turned her head away.

They made two stops en route, one in Israel where she was given a light meal of broth and coffee. From Israel, they were flown by jet to a military base in Germany. While there, Becca learned there had been a discussion on whether or not to fly her and the doctor straight home to the U.S. or hospitalize them there overnight.

At the time, tired, not caring about anything, Becca had no idea who made the decision to fly directly back to the States. Without argument, she ate the light meal she was offered and drank the vitamin-enriched drink handed to her. When finished she settled back and closed her eyes. All she wanted to do was sleep.

And sleep she did, deeply. She roused as the large plane began its descent at another military base near Philadelphia.

Having turned in her sleep, the first thing Becca saw when she opened her eyes was Seth Andrews. He was sound asleep, and asleep he looked like an altogether different man. Though still haggard, in repose the sharp features of his face appeared softer and younger. His enviably long dark lashes blended in with the darkness underlying his eyes.

He looked approachable.

Uh, yeah, Becca chided her fanciful thoughts. She knew better than most how very *unapproachable* Seth Andrews really was. The term *sleeping tiger* sprang to her mind, causing a frown to crease her brow.

The plane's wheels touched down. His eyes sprang open, and he appeared ready to spring to his feet.

"We're landing," she said, her voice rough from her dry throat.

"So I see." He stared at her, hard. "How are you feeling, Rebecca?"

"About as good as anyone after making such a long flight," she answered. "What about you, Doctor? Oh, and everyone calls me Becca," she added, as if he hadn't known that since the first day they had met.

"Matter of fact, Becca, I feel lousy," he admitted, to her surprise. "And, my name, as you well know, is Seth." This statement surprised her even more. "And whether or not you knew it, you were coughing in your sleep."

"I didn't know it." Not about to call him by name, she eyed him warily. The plane was taxiing, somewhere. "Where do we go from here, do you know?"

He nodded wearily. "Yeah. We'll be ambulanced to the U. of P. hospital."

"But…" she protested. "I want to go home. I don't want to go to another hospital."

"Too bad, because you're going." His voice was adamant.

"But…" she began again.

The door of the plane was opened. Hot air rushed into the interior, reminding Becca it was nearing the end of summer in the northeast.

"Save your objections, Becca." He grimaced. "I don't want to go, either. But we're under orders."

"Orders—whose orders?"

The latest crew was coming for them to deplane.

"The head honcho of the hospital," he answered, as she was lifted onto an ambulance gurney. "He wants a complete workup on both of us."

Becca caught the last of his words as she was lowered from the plane.

Damn, she thought, she wanted to go home.

Seth was in a foul mood, not at all happy with the situation. Dammit! He'd screwed up everything. All he had wanted was to get Rebecca out of Africa for her own good.

She coughed as they were sliding the gurney into the ambulance. He frowned. He didn't at all like the sound of that cough. He should have requested rescue for her sooner, even if he had known the administrator of the University of Pennsylvania Hospital would conclude if Rebecca needed to be sent home, in all probability Seth needed a break as well.

Seth had been on staff at the U. of P. for a couple of years before Rebecca had come to work at the hospital. She was one of the best nurses with whom he had ever worked.

She was one of the most lovely and appealing, too. He had felt an attraction to her almost at once— an attraction both physical and emotional that Seth told himself he neither needed nor wanted.

That being the case, he deliberately constructed an invisible shield around himself, a facade of cool detachment and disinterest. Yet, no matter how hard he fought it, the attraction grew stronger. He even tried blaming her, but that wouldn't wash, even to himself, because in all truth, Rebecca had always been efficient, withdrawn and every bit as cool, if not more so.

He hadn't gone to Africa because of her. He was in line to take over for the doctor there within the year she had started at the hospital. But he was relieved when the notice came for him to clear his schedule in preparation for going.

But putting distance between himself and Rebecca hadn't changed his feelings for her in the least. They had grown stronger; he missed her next to him in the O.R., cool detachment or not.

And then, a month after he had arrived in Africa, Becca had shown up to work with him.

He wanted…*wanted*… Well, he sighed, it didn't matter what he wanted.

Rebecca obviously didn't want anything, especially from him.

So, here he was, back in the States, with her and still so far away.

Life sucked.

Two

Two days later, Becca was still in the hospital, in bed, with pneumonia. Her cough had subsided, and yet she still felt weak. As much as she hated to admit it, if only to herself, Dr. Andrews was right in having her shipped home. And she had no intention of admitting it aloud, especially to him.

Seth.

His name swirled inside her mind, along with an image of him as he had looked the last time she had seen him, right before the attendants had slid her gurney into the ambulance.

He hadn't looked good. Becca couldn't help but wonder if he also had pneumonia, or was simply exhausted. Either case was worrisome. It didn't fit with the image she carried in that secret place in her heart.

To Becca, Seth Andrews was the most attractive and sexy man she had ever met. Over six feet tall, lean and rangy, although not as lean as he had grown lately, he exuded a calm self-confidence and a raw sensuality. Becca couldn't have missed the hungry glances he'd received from the other nurses, as well as female doctors, merely by walking along a hospital corridor or stopping by a nurses' station.

And he was the only man she had ever seen with dark-amber eyes. Too bad those eyes never glanced at her with anything other than irritation or impatience.

Becca sighed, thinking it was also too bad she had felt, if not actual love, then a deep infatuation.

She sighed again, afraid the emotion was the former and not the more personally acceptable latter. One hopefully recovered more quickly from infatuation.

Into her disquieting thoughts, Becca was unaware of someone entering the room, until a familiar voice jarred her alert.

"Are you awake?"

Trying to contain the shiver dancing down her spine, Becca reluctantly opened her eyes.

"Yes, I'm awake." She was rather proud of the calm tone she had managed, considering he looked better if not completely well. He had had his hair trimmed, and the wavy mass gleamed in the sunlight that poured into the room.

"How are you feeling?" Coming to a stop beside the bed, he lifted her wrist to take her pulse.

"Rested, a bit stronger," she said, thinking she felt strong enough to gobble him up with a spoon. Shocked by the thought, she quickly asked, "How are you feeling?"

Seth was staring at her blood pressure and heart rate monitor. "A lot better," he said, frowning as he slid his glance from the screen to her face. "Your pulse and heart rate are a little rapid."

Damn. Becca blurted out the first thought to zip through her mind. "I was dozing. You startled me." She held her breath, wondering, hoping he bought her excuse.

"That explains it then." He shot another look at the screen. "Heart rate's leveling." With a flourish, he waved a newspaper in his left hand that she had failed to notice because of her focus on him. "You've made the headlines."

Becca blinked. The headlines? What…? She frowned "I don't understand."

"You're a celebrity," he said, holding the paper up so she could see the article. "At least, you're one below the fold." He handed the folded paper to her, the bottom half displayed.

There it was, under the heading of the article,

her name and a picture of her being carried to the
helicopter on the litter.

Pennsylvania Nurse a Heroine in Africa

Becca quickly scanned the article, then went
back to reread it more carefully. The contents de-
scribed in detail her experience, both in nursing
before volunteering to go to that small village in
Africa, and her service there until she was airlifted
home, exhausted and ill. When she had finished
reading it the second time, she looked up at Seth
Andrews in bewilderment.

"Where?" Shaking her head, she frowned. "How?
Why? Who?" Becca's voice shook with emotion. She
didn't consider herself any kind of heroine.

"I don't know who gave out the story," he said,
anger edging his voice. "I had asked Shakana to
request the transport." A small, cynical smile touched
his tight lips. "I now realize she ratted me out, but I
find it hard to believe she would have alerted the
media, as they say, about you and your condition."

"No, she wouldn't have," Becca said with absolute conviction. "Shakana and I are friends."

"I am and was always well aware of that," he said
in a soothing tone, because it had to be obvious she
was very upset. "No, it was either leaked here or at
the jumping-off site in Israel."

"But the picture was obviously taken in Africa, as I was being lifted onto the helicopter." Becca frowned. "Where did the photographers come from?"

Seth shrugged. "Who knows? It seems these days they are everywhere."

Her frown deepening, Becca looked at the paper again. "I don't like this. I'm not brave. I'm not a heroine." Her voice rose as she slipped into a full rant. "They had no right…now I know how celebrities feel. It's an invasion of privacy, my privacy—"

"Becca…" His voice was low, soothing. It didn't stop her flow of angry words.

"I feel foolish. I'm a nurse, dammit! Nurses are supposed to care for people. If I'm a heroine, then every nurse in the world doing their job is a heroine. I…"

"Becca," he repeated, his voice stronger, almost commanding. She appeared not to hear him.

"I want a retraction," she railed on. "Or at the least, recognition of the good work being done by nurses everywhere." She finally paused to draw breath. Seth struck before she could say another word.

He shut her up very effectively by bending over the bed and covering her mouth with his own.

Becca went stiff at the gentle touch of his lips on hers. Giving a half sigh, half groan, he deepened the kiss as his lips went firm, draining the stiffness from her body and infusing softening warmth.

Becca's body melted against his chest.

Seth slid his arms beneath her to lift her, holding her closer to his hard body.

Her head spinning with sensations, Becca raised her trembling hands to grasp his shoulders, clinging to him, lost in the wonder of the shiver-inducing heat of his mouth, the flicking touch of the tip of tongue. His mouth was demanding, his tongue tormenting.

Within an instant she was hot, burning for him with all the secret passion locked inside her. Tightening her grasp on his arms, she arched in need of getting closer, closer to the heat radiating from him.

A soft cry escaped her when he released her mouth and drew back.

"I'm sorry," Seth said, his voice harsh, his expression stern. Shaking his head, he stepped away from the bed. "That won't happen again." A wry smile eased his tight expression. "It was the only way I could think of to shut you up."

He had kissed her to shut her up? Appalled by his reasoning, Becca could do no more than stare at him.

"You were getting too worked up over the newspaper article. It wasn't good for you in your condition."

And being kissed like there was no tomorrow was good for her? Becca wondered. Blinking in confusion, she refused to recognize or let the tears stinging her eyes fall.

"I'm tired." It was all she could think of to say to him. "I'd like to rest now." There was no way she would admit to him her utter devastation.

For an instant, he looked as if he wanted to say something, then he shrugged and turned away. When he reached the doorway, he glanced back at her. "I'll be back to check on you tomorrow morning."

Becca wanted to protest, call out to him not to stop by, but it was too late. He was gone. She could picture him, striding down the corridor, utterly unaware of the tentative smiles and longing glances sent his way.

Calmer now that Seth was out of the room, Becca replayed in her mind those few magical moments he had held her in his arms, and taken command of her mouth.

She sighed with the same kind of longing so many other women felt for him. And she had thought to call him back, tell him not to stop by the next morning? Ha! She couldn't wait to see him again…fool that she was!

The next moment, Becca frowned. She couldn't believe he had actually explained away his kissing her as the only way he could think of to shut her up. That had to be the most overused, clichéd line in romance fiction. Either the man secretly read too many romance novels, which she seriously doubted, or he had never read any, which she felt certain was the case.

Poor Seth. He didn't even realize he was clichéd and outdated with his approach with women.

Becca couldn't control a small smile at the thought. The sizzling way he kissed, Seth didn't have to worry about his statements being outdated. Hell, he really didn't need to speak at all.

Drowsily, Becca savored the lingering taste of Seth on her lips. His tongue had done a thorough job of teasing the inside of her mouth. The memory triggered a shivery sensation on every nerve ending in her overheated body.

What would making love with him be like?

She quivered at the very idea, before pulling herself together. Get a grip on your imagination, Rebecca, she chided herself in frustration.

Seth Andrews is not interested in you in any personal way. She grimaced. *Matter of fact, he very likely did kiss you to shut you up!*

Damn you. Standing in the corridor not far from Rebecca's room, Seth berated himself for the third, or maybe the fourth time since walking out moments ago. He stared at her chart, as if studying her stats.

What in the world had he been thinking, kissing her the way he had? Admitting to himself he had kissed her because he had wanted to for so long, Seth refused to excuse himself for acting so precipitously. He had had no right to simply grab her and kiss her.

Oh, but she had tasted so good, even with the hint of coffee on her tongue. He had wanted to taste her ever since she had become a member of his surgical team.

And now he had...and almost wished he hadn't. Becca had tasted like heaven, and Seth wanted another taste. No, he wanted to own her mouth, have it for himself alone, have *her* for himself, all to himself.

The mere thought of having Becca, making love to her, shot tongues of fire through Seth's body, directly to the most vulnerable part of his being.

A shudder of hungry desire brought Seth to his senses, to what he was and where he was.

He was a doctor, a surgeon, standing in the hospital corridor fiercely aching for a woman...no, not just any woman, a certain woman.

Rebecca.

Merely thinking her name moved him. He made a half turn to go back into her room, when he caught himself short. What the hell was he doing?

Seth was tempted to laugh. He was driving himself crazy over one kiss, that's what he was doing.

Not too smart, Andrews, he chided himself, as he strode down the corridor, immune to the speculative sidelong glances following his every step.

True to his word, as he always appeared to be, Seth entered her room as Becca was finishing her breakfast. Without asking, he examined the contents of the tray, taking note of what she had eaten.

"You didn't drink your juice."

"I don't like grape juice," she muttered in annoyance. Who did he think he was anyway?

Seth raised his eyebrows and observed wryly, "I see you drank all your coffee."

"I do like coffee." She gave him her sweetest smile. "Matter of fact, I've asked for a second cup."

His gaze lingered on her lips for an extra moment. Becca was hard put not to shiver in response to the heated look she thought she saw in his eyes.

Ridiculous. She rejected the very idea. Seth Andrews giving her a heated look? Yeah, right.

"You have company."

His remark scattered her thoughts, silly as they were. "I have company? Who?" She couldn't imagine. Her parents had retired to a lovely retirement complex in the region around Williamsburg, Virginia. Her sister, Rachael, lived and worked in Atlanta. How would they have known she was back in the States from Africa...?

That damn newspaper article.

"Do you want to see them?"

His voice, now edged with impatience, once again broke into her thoughts.

"Yes, of course I want to see them," she said, every bit as impatiently. "When did they arrive?"

"Yesterday."

Yesterday? Becca frowned. "But, why didn't I see them then?"

"You weren't allowed company yesterday."

"You—"

"No," he said, cutting her off. "Not me. Pulmonary. Dr. Inge decided you needed more time."

Becca sighed. "The head honcho of Pulmonary."

"I see you recall the staff here." He smiled. As slight as it was, his smile went straight to her heart and lungs. She started coughing.

In the next instant, he was pressing the cold stethoscope against her chest. Without speaking, or asking, he lifted her up once again, this time to press the cold instrument to her back.

"Deep breaths."

"I only swallowed the wrong way," she lied, grabbing at the first excuse to enter her empty head.

"Uh-huh, don't talk, deep breaths."

Becca didn't need to be told again; she knew he wouldn't give up until she followed his order.

"Well?" she asked, when he lowered her back onto the bed. "It's clear, isn't it?"

"Yes, fortunately."

She eyed him suspiciously. "Why…fortunately?"

"Because, if there had been the lightest hint of a rustling sound," he answered in a stern tone, "I'd have sent your company packing until tomorrow…maybe."

She heaved a dramatic-sounding, long-suffering sigh. "Since there wasn't, may I see my family now? Please," she muttered through clenched teeth.

"Sure." With that too breezy reply, he sauntered from the room.

If Becca had had something heavy at hand, she'd have hurled it at his head.

Moments later, Seth ushered Becca's parents and sister, Rachael, into the room. "Keep an eye on the time," he said, before walking away.

Becca might have frowned, maybe called out a question to him, but she was caught up in being hugged by her parents and sister, hugging back while tears filled her eyes and overflowed onto her cheeks. As her mother and sister clung to her, her father stood by, holding her hand, as if to say, *I'm here.*

Crying, laughing, everyone spoke at once.

"How did you know…?" Becca began.

"Dr. Andrews called minutes before we saw the article in the paper," her mother answered.

"I learned about it on the TV news, and then Mom called me," Rachael said.

Becca was appalled. "It was on the TV news?"

"Yes." Rachael nodded, grinning. "Prime time, both network and cable." Her grin grew into a quick laugh. "You're a genuine heroine."

"But I'm not," Becca protested. "I'm no more a

heroine than any other nurse." Her voice rose in agitation. "If I'm a heroine, then so are they!"

"Calm down, honey," her father murmured soothingly, squeezing her hand. "Do you want us to get thrown out of here?"

Shocked by his question, Becca glanced up at him as her mother and sister released their hold and stepped back. "Thrown out?" she yelped. "What do you mean? Why would you be thrown out?"

"The good doctor warned us not to upset you," her father said, annoyed. "As if we would deliberately do or say anything to upset you." He stared at her, visibly concerned. "How are you feeling, honey?"

"I'm okay, really," she quickly declared when he appeared skeptical. "I'm still a little tired, but my lungs are clear and I feel okay."

"You look more than a little tired, Rebecca," her mother said, frowning at her.

Becca sighed, but she had to agree. "Yeah, I know. I saw myself in a mirror for the first time this morning. I know I look like death warmed over." And at the time, she had wondered what had prompted Seth to kiss her. She looked a mess. Oh, that's right, she recalled. How could she forget? He kissed her to shut her up.

"Don't even say such a thing," he mother said, bringing Becca's flashing thoughts to a sudden stop.

"What?" She blinked, catching up to what she had said. "Well, it's true, I do look a sorry sight," she defended herself, fighting a grin. She lowered her voice ominously, and said, "Like the face of death."

"Rebecca, that is not funny."

"No?" She gave her mother a wide-eyed, innocent look. "Then why is Dad chuckling, Rachael nearly choking on suppressed laughter, and your lips twitching?"

Her mother tried to look stern, and failed. "You always were a handful," she said, shaking her head as in despair of her youngest.

Her father's chuckle deepened and Rachael lost it, laughing out loud.

"And you weren't much better," her mother said, switching her mock stern look to Rachael.

Rachael laughed harder. Her laughter was contagious and soon her father and Becca joined in. Finally, her mother gave up trying to appear stern and laughed along with the rest of her family.

It was like old times, the four of them laughing together. They had always been a close-knit unit, and it was obvious they loved her as much as Becca loved them.

"We've missed you all these months, Becca," her mother said, her eyes growing misty.

"I missed you, too," Becca replied, feeling the sting in her own eyes.

"Are you going back?" her father asked, always the practical one.

"I'd like to." Becca sighed. "But I really don't believe I'll be allowed to go."

Rachael took her remark personally. "But…why?" she demanded. "Not that we wouldn't miss you just as much as we did before, but I could tell from your letters and e-mails that you loved working there. Why shouldn't you be able to go back when you're fully recovered?"

"I'll tell you why." The low voice came from the doorway.

Becca didn't need to look to see who it was. Only the sound of that one low voice could send chills skating up and down her spine.

"Why then?" Her mother and Rachael turned in unison to confront Seth Andrews, challenge in both their voices. Apparently, her father was prudently going to wait for an answer before he challenged anyone. Becca smiled as he gave her hand another light squeeze.

"Because," Seth calmly answered, "Rebecca is too dedicated or too bullheaded to take care of herself. That's why she was sent home."

"You sent me home," Becca corrected challengingly, swallowing when he slid a look at her.

"You're damn right I did."

Three

The next day, while absently sipping her lunchtime coffee Becca mulled over the events of the day before, most particularly her family's reaction to Seth Andrews's comment about Becca being bullheaded.

Were there angry outcries against his assessment of her? Oh, no, she mused, scowling into her now empty cup. Laughter, each and every one of them. Mother, father and sister agreed with him.

Traitors. The thought wiped the scowl from her lips, replacing it with a smile. It was rather funny, Becca had to agree, at least to herself. Hadn't the three of them been saying the exact same thing, telling her she was bullheaded, since she was in middle school? Truth be told, they had been saying that before she was out of diapers!

Still…they hadn't had to agree with the man, wiseass that he was!

Said wiseass picked that moment to stroll into her room, looking far too attractive for her own good.

"Mail call," he said, holding a cream-colored envelope out to her as he came to stop beside the bed. "And hand delivered, at that."

"Hand delivered?" She was beginning to frown when the light went on in her brain. "Oh, you mean by you."

Shaking his head, as if in despair of her, Seth answered, "No, by a delivery man. You know, the kind of person hired to deliver something."

Condescending jerk, Becca inwardly raged, feeling a need to smack the superior look from his face. But since she was in bed and couldn't reach it, she plucked the envelope from his hand instead.

The very first thing that struck her was the weight and texture of the paper. Expensive stuff, she mused, sliding a fingernail under the flap. Removing the note from the envelope, she quickly scanned it, softly gasped and slowly reread the contents. It began…

Ms. Jameson,
It's my pleasure to inform you that due to

your sacrifice and dedication in giving of your service to the people of Africa, you have been chosen to be awarded by the person to be known as an admirer.

Your award will consist of the use of a fully equipped cabin in the Appalachian Mountains until you are fully recovered or for as long as you wish to stay. Although directions are included, you will be transported to and from your destination. The cabin will be fully supplied, along with a housekeeper/part-time nurse for your care.

We sincerely hope you are well and hearty again soon. Meanwhile, a telephone number is also listed, in case you need anything at all. Please, do not hesitate to call if you do.

That was it, other than a second sheet with the directions.

"Well, damn," Becca muttered, once again reading the missive.

"There's a problem?"

Becca was just getting an inkling that Seth was possibly behind this invitation, but his expression, his tone of voice, doused the idea.

"This is incredible," she answered, frowning down at the sheets of paper in her hand. "I don't know whether to take it seriously or laugh and tear it up."

"May I?" He held his hand out for the letter.

She shrugged. "Sure, why not."

Taking the papers from her, he carefully scanned both sheets before looking at her. "Take it seriously."

"Why should I?"

"I take it you've never heard of the anonymous billionaire?"

"Obviously not," she said, a tad sharply. "But, also obviously, you have. And what does an anonymous billionaire have do to with this letter?" She arched her brows.

He smiled. Well, almost.

"Yes, I have heard of him, but I'm sure whoever it is, he is your benefactor. No one knows who he is, except of course, those who work for him. The person is considered an eccentric, reclusive, generous older man who, in his later years, is sharing the wealth, so to speak."

"Well, naturally, I can't accept this offer."

"Why not?" It was his turn to frown.

"Why not?" she repeated in surprise. "Because it would be like being rewarded for doing my job."

"And...?" Again he pulled that aggravating look of superiority.

"And why should I be?"

Seth leveled an impatient look at her. "Rebecca, you have gone above and beyond the duty of other nurses."

"But…"

He silenced her by simply raising one hand. "I was there, remember? I witnessed your devotion to caring for those people, your genuine affection for them. In the process, you wore yourself out…completely. This generous person is offering you a retreat, a quiet place to rest and rebuild your strength."

Becca was on the verge of protesting once more, but reality intruded. He was right, of course. She was tired, even after several days in bed. The nurse inside her knew she needed more than a week or so to get back to normal.

Besides, she knew Seth, along with her family, would nag her until she agreed.

She let out a soft sigh of defeat. "Okay, I'll go to the mountains," she said, quickly adding, "but only until I feel up to par again."

"Good girl." Seth actually smiled. Amazing. "And you missed a third sheet." He held the paper aloft before handing it to her.

"I did?" Becca frowned, taking the sheet from him. She read the page, then sharply glanced up at him. "This is ridiculous."

"Why?" He arched one eyebrow at her.

She rattled the paper impatiently. "It says a limo will be waiting for me here at the hospital the day I'm released."

"Yes, I read it…so?"

Becca let out a loud sigh. "So…so? So, I have to go home, to my apartment."

"Why?" He raised an eyebrow.

"Why?" she repeated, waving a hand in agitation. "Because I have to pack my things…hell, I need to wash the clothes I brought home with me."

He smiled.

She stifled an impulse to jump from the bed and slug him a good one. "What's so amusing?"

"You are." His smile matured into a grin. "You are very easy to rile. Rebecca, your mother and Rachael can take care of everything."

"Oh." It was stupid—no, it was downright asinine—but damned if she didn't bristle at hearing him say her sister's name. Stupid maybe but… could he possibly feel an attraction to Rachael? Becca smothered an urge to sigh, or cry. She closed her eyes.

It was blatantly obvious Seth Andrews did not feel any kind of an attraction to her, Becca thought, despite that kiss…to shut her up. Why wouldn't he feel an attraction to another woman? Being the eldest, Rachael was beautiful, bright, single and closer to his age. Becca suspected Seth was at least ten years her senior. And, while the difference didn't bother her, it might bother him.

"Hello?" His voice was soft, curious. "Have you fallen asleep on me?"

I wish. Becca shook her head.

His smile vanished, replaced by a look of concern. "Are you feeling all right?"

"I'm a little tired," she said, determined not to admit exactly how tired she felt.

Suddenly he was at the side of her bed, his fingers on the pulse in her wrist, his glance directed to the blood pressure and heart rate monitor to one side.

"I'm okay," she insisted, wanting nothing more than for him to stop touching her. No, what she really wanted was to be swept into his arms for another scorching kiss.

Ain't gonna happen, Becca told herself, except in her dreams.

"Well, your vitals are normal," Seth admitted, gazing down at her in concern. "Do you see now why I insisted you accept that billionaire's offer?" Before she could respond, he added, "The mountains are ideal for resting and recovering. No distractions, fresh air and a housekeeper to take care of you."

"I suppose," Becca said, blinking against the tears misting her eyes. While she knew he was concerned for her as a doctor, she couldn't help feeling he would be happy to see her go.

Her eyelids were losing the blinking battle, so she closed them to staunch the flow. "I think I'd like to take a nap now."

"I think you should."

He didn't move for long seconds. Becca felt sure the gathering tears were about to escape and embarrass her. Finally, she heard the soft swish as he turned and headed to the doorway. "I'll be in later to check on you."

"Umm," she murmured, as if she were half-asleep.

Three days later, Becca was showered, dressed and in a wheelchair, waiting for a nurse to wheel her to the exit where the limo would be waiting for her.

She was tired, from the shower and dressing, she told herself. And though she felt a bit depressed, she told herself it had nothing to do with not having seen Seth in three days.

Becca firmed her lips into a flat, determined line. She would not allow herself to go into a blue funk over an arrogant, overbearing…absolutely wonderful man. Uhh, scratch the last adjective.

As if summoned by her thoughts, the man haunting her dreams strolled into her room.

"Ready to go, I see," Seth said, coming to a halt mere inches from her chair.

"Waiting for someone to wheel me down," Becca said, somehow managing to sound cheery…when all she really wanted to do was weep, and tell him she didn't want to go.

"It may be a few minutes. I understand the staff is very busy." He simply stood there, looking at her, so close, yet so far away.

For a minute.

Becca stopped thinking, breathing, when he leaned forward over her. He placed his hands on the armrests of the wheelchair, to lean closer.

"Wha…wha…" she muttered, unable to force the full word from her suddenly parched throat.

"You will let the housekeeper take care of you," he said, so close now his breath whispered over her lips, causing havoc in every cell she possessed.

Beyond speech, Becca nodded.

"Good." He smiled; she smelled mint on his breath, and yearned to taste it. "I'll miss you in the O.R."

Becca deflated like a pierced balloon. Of course, hadn't he at one time admitted she was the best O.R. nurse he had ever worked with?

She shut her eyes in private misery, and wasn't aware of him closing the inches between them. The touch of his lips on hers startled her and set her pulse pounding.

Seth's kiss was soft, gentle, undemanding and heart-wrenchingly sweet. Within a moment, before she could even think to respond, he moved away.

Becca lowered her head and her lashes.

With the tip of his finger, he tilted her face up to

meet his steady gaze. His amber eyes had darkened to a shade of brown she had not seen before.

"Get well," he said. "Take care of yourself, little girl."

Girl? Little girl!

A wave of anger crashed over Becca, washing away her misery along with her caution and good sense.

"Little girl," she protested, her voice elevated. "I'm not a little girl, Doctor. I'm a woman."

"Tell me about it."

As he finished speaking, a nurse breezed into the room, distracting Becca from wondering about the odd note in his quiet voice, the flash of emotion in his now dark eyes.

"Hi, I'm Jen, sorry to keep you waiting," the young woman said, bending to flip the locks from the chair's wheels. "It's been a busy day." Smiling, she moved to the back of the chair. "Ready to go? Your chariot awaits outside."

Seth stepped back as Jen rolled the chair to the doorway. "Doctor," she said politely, smiling as she moved past him and started down the corridor.

"Come back healthy, Rebecca. I need you…in the O.R."

Seth's quiet voice floated down the corridor after her.

Clutching the chair arms, she fought against the

sting in her eyes. She had known all along he wasn't interested in her in any personal way. She was a good O.R. nurse.

No! she thought, lifting her head and angling her jaw. She was a terrific O.R. nurse. And when she was completely back up to speed, she silently vowed, she would not torture herself by returning to work for him.

Maybe.

When Jen rolled the chair outside the electric doors, Becca couldn't get out of the chair and into the impressive black stretch limo fast enough. She did not look back.

Seth stood rigid behind the large, heavy plate-glass door. A strange sensation invaded his stomach—emptiness? He shrugged the thought aside.

He didn't have time to worry about a stubborn woman. He didn't really need her in the O.R.; there were plenty of good—no, excellent—nurses waiting, hoping to take her place.

Yet he didn't move away from the door. He stood there, watching until after she had disappeared inside the limo. Hell, he was missing her already and the car hadn't yet pulled away from the building.

Becca. A pang in his chest startled him.

Dammit, she never so much as glanced back.

* * *

In a word, the limousine was plush. There was a small cooler holding snacks, and a bar with an ice-filled bucket chilling a bottle of champagne.

Curious, and hungry, as the lunch carts had just started to be pushed along the hospital corridor as she was being wheeled out, Becca investigated the bounty. Caviar, she marveled, the outrageously expensive stuff.

Expensive but gross, she thought, making a face. Thankfully there were several different kinds of cheeses and crackers and a bunch of plump black grapes. Yum, that was more like it.

Popping the cork on the bottle, she poured the golden, bubbly liquid into a real crystal flute and made a meal of the cheese, crackers, fruit and champagne…three glasses of champagne.

After sealing what was left of the champagne with the foil cap and packing away the remains of the food, Becca made herself comfortable by curling up on the butter-soft seat and promptly fell asleep.

Becca didn't know where she was; the setting was lush but unfamiliar. She was in a freshwater pool, serenely floating naked in the cool water.

It was a peaceful, quiet place, a secret bower with heavy foliage and masses of bright-hued flowers on the banks surrounding the pool. And there was a waterfall, a gentle flow cascading into the sparkling water.

Lovely. She was alone but unafraid, somehow knowing this was where she belonged.

There came a splash, not loud, but as if a fish had leapt with joy in the pool. Small ripples blurred the water, drawing closer to her.

The next instant he was there, his lean bare body gliding along hers.

"Seth." Her eyes closing, she breathed his name, as if she had known he would be there.

"Yes." His lips were close to her ear. "Have you been waiting long?"

"Forever," she murmured against his jaw.

"I'm here now…for you." A slight turn of his head and his mouth took hers. A gentle, tender kiss, for a moment.

Becca curled her wet arms around his neck, and arched her body into his, murmuring low in her throat when he deepened the kiss, taking complete command of her mouth with his lips and tongue.

Without thought, she lifted her legs and coiled them around his hips, feeling the strength of his need, and loving the feel of it.

"You want me," he whispered against her lips.

"Yes…" she sighed, arching higher into him. "Yes, please."

"Then I'm yours." He moved into position between her legs. She felt him there, and...

"Ms. Jameson."

The soft, unfamiliar voice broke the spell. Becca opened her eyes, and nearly cried out in protest.

She was lying on the seat of the unmoving limo. She raised her eyes to see the driver, his expression both concerned and compassionate.

"We're here, at the cabin." He smiled. "Sorry to have to wake you. You were sleeping pretty soundly."

"Yes," she said, blinking herself fully awake and aware.

"I—" she began, only to have him interrupt.

"You obviously needed the rest," he said, getting out of the car to open the door for her.

She needed something, Becca thought wryly, and right that minute rest didn't come close.

"Well, there you are," a voice called out, startling Becca. "And just in time for supper, too."

Becca looked up at the woman standing on the wide porch running along the entire front of the...cabin? Ha! This place was the last thing Becca would call a cabin. The word *resort* jumped into her mind.

"Come on in, honey, and get acquainted. I'm Sue Ann, but folks just call me Sue."

"Hi, Sue," Becca said, stepping out of the car and mounting the four steps to the porch. She held out her hand. "I'm Rebecca." She smiled. "But folks just call me Becca."

Sue returned the smile, and turned to the driver, who stood patiently waiting at the base of the steps, his hands full of Becca's luggage.

"I'm Dan," he offered. "Sorry I can't shake your hand, ma'am."

"My name's Sue," she said, laughing. "And you two come right on inside."

Becca liked the woman at once. In her mid-fifties, Becca judged, nice, down-to-earth, the solid type.

"I'll show you to the room I've prepared for you," she said, striding to a hallway and motioning Becca and Dan to follow. "'Course, if it don't suit, you have your choice of any of the four others."

"Only five bedrooms?" Becca said, laughing. "What kind of cheap dump have I been subjected to?"

Dan chuckled.

Sue laughed along with Becca. "Yeah, shame, ain't it?" She swung open a door. "You'll just have to rough it for a while, I suppose."

Becca caught her breath as she stepped into the room. It was simply gorgeous, luxurious, downright, flat-out decadent. A room fit for royalty.

"Sheesh," Becca whispered in awe.

"Think you might be able to make do?" Sue asked, in mock concern.

Becca nodded. "Yeah, for a while, at least."

Laughing, Sue headed from the room. "Just drop the bags, Dan. I'll take care of them later." She glanced at Becca. "Why don't you freshen up, then come out to the kitchen, before supper dries up. You, too, Dan."

Dan thanked her, but demurred. "I'd better to be on my way, ma'am."

"You not going to drive all the way back tonight, are you?" Becca said.

He shook his head. "No, just an hour or two. All the arrangements have been made for me. Matter of fact, I think I'll be going, while it's still light."

Impulsively, Becca hugged him as she thanked him. Within minutes the limo was smoothly moving away from the house.

"Well, then," Sue said. "Let's you and I get to know each other over supper."

Four

The first week at the so-called cabin went well for Becca. Sue appeared determined to spoil her rotten. Surprisingly, independent as she always had been, Becca reveled in the pampering. Sue insisted she rest, so Becca rested. Sue insisted she eat, so Becca ate…and very well, too.

On her first full day there, Becca unpacked, delighted to see Rachael had stowed her laptop and several novels in her cases, along with plenty of clothing. After putting everything neatly away, she had lunch and then a nap. Later, she explored the house, and was not surprised to find that every room was as beautifully decorated as her bedroom, if not as luxuriously. Obviously, she figured her room was the master suite.

Two days later, she felt quite at home, and was already fond of Sue. But then, she thought, who wouldn't be? Sue zipped about like a teenager. And she was one terrific companion, not to mention a great cook. Becca was certain she would be a lot heavier when she left the cabin than when she arrived.

Once she'd gotten comfortable at the cabin, she began exploring the outdoors, starting with the long porch. From the position of the house halfway up a foothill, Becca could see a town nestled in a narrow valley below. Curious, she brought up the subject of the town over supper.

Sue was happy to give Becca a short history of the town, named Forest Hills, for obvious reasons. There were a lot of forested hills, not to mention mountains completely surrounding it.

"That town dates back to the eighteen eighties," Sue began. "It started up when veins of coal were discovered."

Sue paused, and Becca inserted, "I didn't see anything while on the porch that looked like a mine."

"That's 'cause you can't see it from here," she said. "It's located in a fold of the mountains nine or so miles from here." She smiled, sipped her tea and said, "I was born in this town. My ancestors settled here before it was a town. They were farmers, heading west, this little valley looked good to them. So they stayed, settled. We've been here ever since."

Becca took the opportunity to ask another question when Sue took another sip of tea.

"You've lived here all your life?"

"Lord, no," she replied with a quick head shake. "I shook the dust of this place off my shoes right after I graduated high school. I went to the city to college to become a nurse."

"Really?" Becca smiled. "That had to take courage. I mean, growing up in a small town, then going off alone to a big city." She hesitated, but asked outright, "Did you make it—the nursing, I mean?"

Sue gave a proud smile. "Sure I made it, even got my bachelor's degree in science."

"Good for you. That's wonderful." Becca returned a small shy smile. "I did, too."

"Oh, honey, I know," Sue said, giving her a thumbs-up. "I know all about your work in Africa, too. I hear you almost worked yourself right into the ground."

Sighing, Becca shook her head. "No such thing."

Sue pulled a skeptical expression. "That isn't the way I heard it."

"Overplayed by the media." Becca shrugged.

So it was all well and good—for the first week. There was one little problem with Becca: she continued to dream about Seth every night, erotic fantasies that made her blush come morning. Night after night, in each dream, she was alone and naked, always in a beautiful but different setting than the first. In every dream, he was suddenly there.

They would not talk. His naked, slim, muscular body was impressive in full arousal. Becca would open her arms to him at once, and he would lie next to her, holding her, his hands caressing her, his mouth tormenting her. In desperation, she would tug at his hair, his shoulders, urging him closer, closer. He'd murmur without speaking, and move sensuously between her thighs. His tongue would thrust deep into her mouth, drawing a moan of need from her throat into his. His mouth and tongue owning hers, he'd move and…

Becca would awaken, her breathing ragged, her body moist all over, longing, longing. Frustration became her constant companion.

She wanted…she wanted…Seth—all of him.

Toward the middle of the second week she confided to Sue some of her restlessness. She wasn't about to describe her dreams. She was embarrassed even thinking about them. Not that she wanted them to end. Oh, no. Since she knew the dreams were all she would probably ever have of him, she cherished each and every one…but her frustration grew. It had been a long time—back to her college days, in fact—since she had been intimate with a man. The experience had not been earth-shattering.

"I'm getting antsy sitting around here," she said, between bites of a delicious stew. She was almost amused by the understatement.

"No kidding," Sue said, rolling her eyes. "I'd have never known, if not for seeing you prowling back and forth like a caged animal." She grinned.

Becca grinned back. "Can I help with your work, if only a little?"

"Absolutely not," Sue said resolutely. "I'm getting paid for taking care of this place and you, and paid very nicely, thank you."

Becca's shoulders drooped. "Oh, well, I might as well pack up and leave. I'll go flaky with nothing to do. I'm getting cabin fever already."

"Weeelll," Sue began, pausing as she got up to pour coffee for both of them. "Maybe I can help you find something light to do."

"The dusting?" Becca asked eagerly, accepting the steaming cup.

Sue shook her head. "No, I told you, this place is my job for now. But…"

"But?" Becca prompted.

"I have another job, part-time, and I was thinking you might be able to help there."

"Where?" Becca asked, and immediately added, "Doing what and with whom?"

"Nursing." Sue paused for a reaction. She got it as the word left her lips.

"Nursing, where?"

"At the small clinic in town."

"I didn't know there was a clinic in town." Becca was anxious to hear more. "Tell me about it."

"First let me give you a thumbnail background." She slid her soup plate aside and cradled her coffee cup in her palms. "The clinic is run by Dr. John Carter. He was raised here—I've know him most of my life. John was ahead of me in school. Like me, he left after graduating high school to attend college, followed by med school."

She took a tentative sip of her drink before going on. "Unlike me, he came back here to set up a practice. He's been serving the community ever since."

"And you work for him?"

Sue nodded. "On a part-time basis."

Becca frowned. "But you said something about a clinic. Where does that come in?"

Sue laughed at her eager tone. "There were times, accidents and such, when John's small office was overcrowded with hurt or sick people. There were a few times with mine accidents when it was chaos. You see, the nearest hospital is over a half an hour away."

"But that means…" Becca began, appalled.

"Yes," Sue nodded. "Some men died in transit." She drew a breath and took a swallow of coffee. "So, ten or so years ago, the mine owner paid to have an addition attached to John's building, which he owns and lives in, in the apartment above. I must admit, the owner, Carl Dengler, didn't skimp. The clinic is well-equipped, not state-of-the-art, but good. John does X-rays and blood work. Everything except surgery. It has saved more than a few lives."

"Oh, my gosh!" Becca said. "That's right up my alley."

Sue smiled. "That's what I thought."

"When can I go to meet Dr. Carter?"

"How 'bout tomorrow morning?"

"Yes!" Becca punched the air. "Please."

Two days later, Becca was back to doing the work she loved. No, it wasn't the precision work of being next to Seth in the O.R., but it was satisfying nonetheless. Best of all, it kept her mind engaged and busy, as well as her hands. The edge was taken off her frustration.

Becca liked Dr. Carter at once. Nearing sixty, he was still in excellent physical shape, and still handsome. She could just imagine how attractive he must have been to the female population when he was young.

He appeared to live alone, as Becca heard no mention of a wife, nor was introduced to anyone.

Curious, she asked Sue about his possible marital status.

She was happy to clarify. "John married his college sweetheart right after graduation. He brought her home with him. Apparently, she had other dreams of life being married to a doctor. She lasted not quite two years, then she packed up and left." She grimaced. "So far as anyone knows, except to sign the divorce papers her lawyer mailed him, John hasn't heard a word from her since."

"And no local lady friend?"

"Oh," Sue said. "John has lots of female and male friends, but no lady friend in the way you mean."

"Skittish, huh?"

"Yeah, and it's a shame. He's a great guy." Sue sighed and walked away, ending the discussion.

Becca watched her, curious. Her sigh had not only a note of compassion, but a touch of longing as well. Hmm, she thought, interesting.

As Sue had explained Becca's situation to John, he agreed to her working three half days a week to begin. She was tempted to argue for more time, but gave in gracefully, as she somehow knew she wouldn't win, anyway.

By Saturday, working her third half day of the week, Becca had settled in as if she had worked in the small clinic for years. She was back in form and loving it.

* * *

It was hot and humid in Philadelphia. Summer was hanging on to the east coast like a leech to a blood vessel. There were frequent storms; with each one, the air seemed to get hotter and more humid.

Seth was tired. He was tired of the heat. He was tired of the humidity. He was damn sick of feeling tired. He knew most of his problem was mental, not physical.

Physically, Seth was feeling pretty good. He wasn't back to performing surgery yet, but he had been helping his practice partner, Colin Neil, by doing hospital rounds checking on the progress of Colin's pre- and post-surgical patients.

No, the problem wasn't physical…except in one particular and vulnerable part of his body. But, sexual frustration aside, his health was much better than when he had left Africa weeks ago.

Truth to tell, Seth felt fine as long as he was inside the hospital. Talking to patients, checking charts, reading test results along with discussing individual patients with Colin kept him too busy to think or brood about other, personal matters.

Actually, there was only one matter, and that matter's name was Becca. The moment he stepped through the hospital doors at the end of the day, her name filled his mind and senses.

Thinking about her, wondering about her—how

she was feeling, what she was doing, who she might be meeting—was driving him nuts. And underneath the relentless, nagging thoughts was an emotion he refused to recognize.

Seth had tried evasive action. He did something he had never done before. He had dated another doctor. Her name was Kristi and she was doing her internship. He had agreed to let her trail behind him, observe as he did his daily rounds.

That had been a few days after Becca had left. Seth had hoped having an intern with him, answering her questions, explaining his and Colin's procedure, might keep his mind centered.

And it had worked, so well that he figured if it worked during the day, maybe…

Anyway, Seth had asked Kristi out to dinner. She didn't so much as hesitate—she said yes immediately.

All well and good, Seth figured. They could share a nice dinner and possibly, very probably, some professional conversation. He fully expected her to pick his brain, and why not? He didn't mind.

Kristi was a very attractive woman. Any man would be proud to be seen with her. She was pretty, slender and petite, very feminine.

She was also very bright, which was what appealed to Seth even more than her looks. In his opinion, she would make an excellent physician. In addition, she had a good sense of humor. All and all, Seth found her a wonderful dinner and conversational companion.

On seeing her home, Seth had even kissed her, not a friendly peck but a real kiss.

He felt nothing.

Oh, it wasn't horrible or even unpleasant. But it was bland, ho-hum, not at all the shockingly erotic physical and emotional impact he had experienced when he had kissed Becca.

Dammit.

It wasn't her fault. Kristi simply wasn't Becca. The most ridiculous part was he had actually felt as if he had cheated on Becca.

Talk about being tired.

He missed Becca and Seth was, in a word, miserable. Still, he soldiered on, making rounds, checking charts, answering Kristi's questions.

Seth lasted until near the end of the third week after Becca left. Then he caved to the urge gnawing inside him. He had to see her, be convinced she was taking care of herself, resting, eating, getting well.

On Friday of that week, he told Colin he would be leaving town for an end-of-summer vacation, and that hopefully he would be ready to go back into active practice when he returned. His partner agreed it was an excellent idea, and that he'd hold down the fort…so to speak.

Packing enough clothes to last about a week, Seth set out for West Virginia near dawn on Saturday morning.

The trip was long and tedious, with a short break for breakfast. Finally, around lunchtime, he brought his car to a stop at the cabin. Some cabin, Seth thought, shaking his head in near disbelief at the beautiful structure. But then, it belonged to a billionaire, he should have suspected more than a mere cabin in the woods.

Leaving the car, he mounted the steps to the wide porch and knocked at the solid oak door. The door opened to reveal a sober-faced, middle-aged woman.

"Yes?" Her eyebrows rose.

Seth smiled. "Hi, I'm Seth Andrews. I'm looking for Rebecca Jameson," he said. "Is she here?"

"You're Dr. Andrews," she said, smiling back. "Becca didn't say she was expecting you."

A funny sensation trickled through him. "Has she mentioned me?"

"Oh, yes." She nodded. "Said you worked together in Africa."

"That's right…and before Africa." He frowned. "Isn't she here?"

"Oh…my goodness, where are my manners," she said, sounding flustered. "My name is Sue, I'm the housekeeper. Come in, Doctor, come in." She stepped back, swinging the door wide.

Once inside the lovely room, Seth tried again. "Is Becca here?"

"No, she isn't," Sue answered. "She's working."

For an instant, everything stopped cold inside Seth. He arched his brows. "Working?" He had to work to keep his voice calm. "Where is she working?"

"She's helping out part-time with our doctor at the clinic in town." She glanced at her watch. "Matter of fact, I was about ready to go pick her up."

"I'll go," Seth quickly offered. "If you can point me in the right direction?"

"Oh, it's easy to find," Sue said, grinning. "Fact is, it's hard to miss. You follow the road at the other side of the house down the hill to town, it's called Forest Hills, the clinic is right along West Street, the main drag."

"Thank you, Sue." He turned to leave. She brought him to a stop at the door.

"Dr. Andrews, have you come to take Becca home?" Sue's voice had a note of disappointment.

He looked back to offer her a wry smile. "Only if she is ready to go, Sue. It's up to her." Without waiting for a possible response, he opened the door and walked out.

Working. *Working.* Seth fumed and sped down the winding road as if there were no tomorrow.

Dammit, had the woman completely lost her mind? He barely felt ready to go back to work, and she had been in a lot worse shape than him.

Seth found the clinic easily, just as Sue said he would. He found a parking space along the curb, then walked to the nondescript building and stepped inside. The first thing he saw was the back of Becca.

She was slightly bent over a woman who appeared to be weeping. He hesitated, waiting until she turned to walk to a door set in the far wall next to a reception desk, unattended at the moment.

When she opened the door and stepped through, he followed her, sparing a concerned frown for the softly crying woman.

Following Becca through the door, he saw her, shoulders slightly drooping, about to enter another door farther along a hallway. Even in profile, he could see the tension on her face, the tired, anxious look.

Exasperation immediately turned to impatience. Searing anger spiraled through Seth's entire being. Without thinking, he snapped at her.

"What the hell are you doing?"

Five

For an instant, Becca froze in surprise and shock at the sharp sound of Seth's voice. The sensation swiftly changed into a quick burst of joy inside at the reality of him being there. Then the present reality intruded.

As mere moments passed, she kept her hand curled around the doorknob and turned to scowl at him.

"I don't have time for this, Doctor," she said, anger rising to replace all other feelings. "There's a young boy choking in here."

Turning the knob, she entered the room, fully aware Seth was right behind her. Dr. Carter stood next to the examining table, on which a boy lay unconscious and gasping for every breath. The doctor was very carefully working a breathing tube down the boy's nasal passage.

"Foreign object?" Seth quietly asked from where he had come to a stop right beside her.

"No." Becca shook her head. "Allergic reaction to a bee sting."

"Have you administered epinephrine?"

"No," she repeated. "The doctor's receptionist is looking for—"

"Becca, who is this man, and what's he doing in here?" Dr. Carter interrupted. He didn't look up from the boy, but his tone gave clear indication of his impatience.

"The name's Seth Andrews, I'm also a physician. I worked with Rebecca in Africa."

Dr. Carter gave Seth a quick glance.

"Have you called for an ambulance?" Seth asked, keeping his gaze on the boy. "He's still struggling to breathe. He should be in a hospital."

"I agree." John sighed. "Problem is the closest hospital is over a half hour away. He wouldn't have made it there."

"Not without the epinephrine," Seth responded caustically. "Why is there none available?"

"Becca told you my receptionist is looking for one." His tone was sharp. "And I'm beginning to panic here, as I can't get this tube any deeper."

This entire exchange lasted no more than a few

seconds, during which Becca had moved to stand beside the doctor in case he needed her. Both she and John looked up when Seth spoke again.

"He's not getting enough air," he said urgently. "He needs a tracheotomy…now, or there could be brain damage."

John's eyes widened and his face drained of color. "I never…I'm not a surgeon…" He glanced at the boy, swallowed, straightened his shoulders and said, "But I'll do my best."

"I am a surgeon, and while I've never performed this procedure, I know how it's done," Seth said. "Would you prefer I do it?"

"Please."

"Is he sedated or did he pass out?"

"Passed out," John answered. "He was terrified."

Seth nodded. "Where can I scrub?"

"There's a sink behind you." John inclined his head.

Seth turned, saying, "Becca."

That's all he had to say. Becca got busy. By the time Seth turned from the sink, with his hands up, she was masked. She held a lab coat out and he straightened his arms for her to slide it on backwards. Moving behind him, she closed two buttons to hold the makeshift scrub top in place. The next second she was shoving plastic gloves onto his hands, and tying a mask on his face.

"Anesthetic?"

"I've administered a low dose," John said. "We don't need another reaction."

Seth nodded, and without saying another word, or asking any more questions, he moved to the side of the examining table, as if he knew without doubt Becca would have everything he needed prepared for him to begin.

And, of course, she did. Still not speaking or looking at her, he held out his right hand. Becca slapped a scalpel into his palm.

Concentrating on the job at hand, Becca was still vaguely aware of a light tap on the door, the quiet voice of Mary, the receptionist, saying, "I found it, Doctor," and John's equally soft voice thanking her. He then told her to call at once for an ambulance, and also said to tell the boy's mother he would be all right.

In short order, working with his accustomed precision, Seth set aside the instrument and inserted the breathing tube Becca handed to him into the child's trachea. The boy's breathing eased noticeably at once and slowly returned to a normal pattern. John handed the syringe to her and she plunged the needle into the boy.

As Seth stepped back, away from the table, another tap sounded on the door, and a voice said, "Ambulance crew."

Glancing at John, Seth said, "He's about ready to go."

With her usual calm efficiency, Becca dressed the wound around the tube. Just then, the boy's eyelids fluttered and opened. She smiled into his startling and blessedly clear green eyes.

"Mommy," the child cried in a rough whisper.

"I'm here." Tears streaming down her face, the woman from the waiting room shouldered her way by the ambulance crew. "I'm here, baby, Mommy's here."

While the crew gently slid the child from the table to their litter, the woman grabbed John's hands. "Thank you, Doctor, thank you so very…"

"I did very little, it's Dr. Andrews you should thank." He turned her to face Seth.

She repeated her gratitude to Seth, and impulsively grabbed and hugged him.

Not unused to being hugged by grateful patients and family members, Seth patted the woman's back gently. "You're welcome, now go with your boy."

With tears still trickling down her face, she gave him a brilliant smile and rushed after the ambulance crew.

Becca felt misty-eyed but exhilarated…for all of three or four minutes. Then she crashed. Exhaustion, part physical but mostly emotional, struck like a blow. With a last surge of energy, she pulled off the lab coat and the mask from her face. Heaving a heavy sigh, she dropped like a stone onto the chair at the doctor's small desk.

Seth heard her sigh and he turned to give her a probing look, in exactly the same piercing way he would gaze at one of his still shaky patients.

"You look beat." His tone was not kind, more accusing. "You shouldn't be working yet. It's obvious you aren't strong enough."

"I'm okay," she insisted, abruptly standing to prove her point. For a second the room spun around her and her stomach lurched, proving only that she was completely played out.

"Right." Seth shook his head, showing his impatience with her. "Let's go."

"I can't go now," she protested, feeling the need to sit down again. "I have to clean up in—"

"Seth is right, Becca, you've done more than enough for one day," John interrupted. "You look about ready to collapse. Mary and I will do the cleaning up."

"But—" Becca began once again, and again she was interrupted, this time by Seth.

"Don't argue," he said, moving to her to gently but firmly take hold of her arm. "And be still," he went on as she tried to shake his arm off.

In truth, Becca was too tired to argue. She allowed Seth to lead her from the clinic to his car.

It was a nice one, too, and expensive. But she was even too tired to comment on the vehicle.

Becca nearly fell asleep on the drive back to the cabin. Fortunately, she thought, as she roused with a start when the car came to a halt at the house, she hadn't drifted deep enough for her to dream.

The very idea of Seth witnessing her in the throes of one of her erotic dreams was embarrassing. Whatever would he think? She didn't want to find out.

Seth was out of the car and at her door before Becca finished undoing her seat belt. Pulling the door open, he again took her arm, guiding her from the car and up the porch steps.

The door swept open, revealing a concerned-looking Sue. "What happened, Becca? You look awful." She leveled a narrow-eyed look at Seth. "What have you done to her? You, of all people…" That's as far as Seth let her get.

"She's all right," he said, brushing past her to lead Becca inside to a chair. "There was an emergency at the clinic. A child stung by a bee had an allergic reaction. He was asphyxiating when I got there."

Sue's eyes widened and her one hand flew to her chest. "Oh, my lord," she exclaimed. "Is he…" She paused, as if afraid to voice her fear.

"No." Seth shook his head to reassure the woman, but kept his intent gaze on Becca, who had her eyes closed and was resting her head against the back of the deeply padded chair. "He'll be fine. He's being ambulanced to the hospital."

"Thank goodness," Sue murmured, her anxious gaze also fixed on Becca. "She overdid it, didn't she?"

"What else?" Seth's tone was wry. "I believe she thinks she's indestructible...but..." He hesitated before adding, "She was magnificent."

Becca blinked her eyes open. "I was no such thing," she protested, scowling at him. "I didn't perform the surgery."

"Surgery?" Sue jumped on the word. "John performed surgery on the boy?"

Becca shook her head. "No, no, Sue. Seth did it, although John was prepared to do it."

"But John's not a surgeon!" Sue said.

"That's why I did it," Seth inserted. "I am a surgeon. But John would have tried."

"Of course he would," Sue agreed. "John is a devoted, caring..." The ringing of the phone stopped her cold. "I'll get it," she said, turning away.

"Is there any coffee, Sue?" Becca called after her. "I think I need a shot of caffeine."

"Yes," Sue called back. "I made a pot for lunch, but I'll make a fresh pot as soon—"

"No, I'll get it," Becca said, interrupting.

"No, I'll get it," Seth interrupted Becca. "You stay here and rest. Where's the kitchen?"

"Follow me," Sue said from the dining room. "That's where I'm going."

"But…" Becca started to rise.

"Sit down and behave yourself," Seth ordered, in his most I'm-the-boss tone, as he strode after the housekeeper.

Watching the back of his retreating form, Becca began to simmer. That…that…*man,* she thought. Who the hell did he think he was? Well, she continued in her mental rant, she wasn't about to let him order her around. She no longer worked for him. He was not her boss.

Carefully rising, Becca stood still a moment. When her head didn't whirl, or her stomach rebel, she smiled. Moving slowly, she took one step, then another. Ha! She could walk just fine. *Take that, Mister-Big-Deal-I'm-The-Man-Surgeon.*

Feeling proud of herself, which she admitted to herself was pretty childish, Becca sauntered through the dining room to the kitchen. Seth was standing at the countertop, pouring coffee into two mugs.

"You take orders much better in the O.R.," he grumbled, turning to carry the mugs to the table.

"But we're not in the O.R.," Becca said, calmly, seating herself, "are we?"

He raised his incredible amber eyes.

She met his steady stare head-on.

Standoff?

"Doesn't matter," he said, after a long moment. Turning, he went to the fridge to get milk. "Considering your condition, I'm still in command." Giving her a wry smile, he set the carton of milk on the table. "Do you use sugar?" As if he didn't know.

"No, and what do you mean by my condition?" Becca asked, stunned by his blatant assumption. "What condition?" she stormed, in attack mode. "I'm a little tired. I'll be fine. In fact, I'm feeling better already." She pulled a cheery smile, but felt it didn't quite come off. "That's all there is to it. End of story."

During their strained exchange, Becca could hear Sue talking on the phone, even though she couldn't make out her words. Then she heard Sue cradle the instrument.

"Becca...I have sandwiches and a salad prepared and in the fridge for lunch," Sue said in a rush as she approached the table. "And a chicken vegetable pie ready to go into the oven for supper." She hesitated, smiled and rushed on. "Dr. Carter wants to see me...would it be all right with you if I went out for the night?"

Becca was already nodding her head, a smile shadowing her lips, certain Sue's sudden attack of nerves could be attributed to John's invitation...for the night, perhaps? The shadow materialized into a real smile at the thought. She had guessed Sue and

John were interested in each other, and both were tiptoeing around making a bold move.

"Of course, I don't mind. I'm tired, Sue, not half-dead. I'll be fine."

"Oh, thanks, sweetie." Sue actually beamed. "I'll just get my purse and—"

"Sue, wait a moment, please," Seth said, interrupting her. "Before you leave, can you direct me to the closest motel or rooming house?"

"Rooming house!" Sue exclaimed. "Motel? I'll do no such thing." She swept the area with one arm. "Here's this big house, and you're thinking rooming house? Becca has the master suite down here, but there are four empty bedrooms upstairs." She paused to breathe.

Becca jumped in. "Uh, Sue, I don't think—"

"Now don't tell me the owner will mind, honey," Sue interrupted. "What that rich man doesn't know won't be hurting anyone."

She glanced at Seth, who, to Becca's way of thinking, appeared much too innocent-looking. "Now, before I leave, you go right out and get your gear from the car, then I'll show you the place and you can take your pick of the rooms…all with their own bathroom, I might add."

"Well…if you insist."

Becca gritted her teeth at the humble note in his voice.

"I do." Sue gave a definite nod of her head. "No, *we* do. Don't we, Becca?"

No! Becca kept her lips tightly closed to contain the word of denial from bursting out of her mouth. "Yes," she agreed, not too graciously. "We do."

Seth smiled.

Had Becca been closer to him she might have smacked that victorious smile from his face. Wanting only to put some distance between them before she did something rash like face-smacking, she said, "Why don't you get your bags so Sue can be on her way?"

He nodded, smile still in place. "Right." Moving smartly, he headed for the door.

Becca heaved a soft sigh of relief. Still, Sue heard it. "You're still tired. Why don't you lie down for a bit? The sandwiches and salad will keep."

"I'm fine, honestly." This time Becca's smile was genuine. "I promise if I start to feel any worse, I'll rest."

Sue smiled back. "Okay, and it might help if you'd eat a little something."

"That sounds good to me," Seth chimed in, strolling into the kitchen, suitcase in hand. "I haven't eaten since early this morning."

Hanging on to her fraying composure, Becca rose from the table, carrying the still full coffee cup. "Okay, you get settled in and I'll serve lunch."

"Good," Sue said, heading for the archway into the dining room. "Follow me, Seth. I'm sure Mr. Moneybags won't mind how long you stay."

Oh, hell...hell...hell! Becca railed to herself. *Just stay as long as you like, Seth. Have yourself a great time driving Becca to distraction.*

Fuming, she dumped the now cold, bitter coffee into the sink and fixed a fresh pot. While the coffee brewed, she set about slapping place mats and napkins on the table, followed by plates for the sandwiches and small wooden bowls for the salads. She was setting the large bowl of mixed vegetable salad onto the table when Sue hurried back into the room.

"Seth will be down in a minute," she said, grabbing her purse and heading for the door. "I'll be leaving now...okay?"

"Yes, of course—go, Sue." Becca made a shooing motion with her hand, managing a smile for her. "I'll be fine. Dr. Carter is waiting."

"Right." Excitement glimmered in Sue's eyes. "Uh...I don't know when I'll be..."

"Don't worry about it," Seth drawled, sauntering into the room. "I assure you, I'll take good care of her."

Sue grinned, and rushed out of the house.

Becca was simmering. Who in the world assigned Seth Andrews, boy-wonder surgeon, to take care of her? She was fully capable of taking care of herself, thank you.

Carefully setting the sandwiches on the plates, she tried to calm her rising ire, afraid if she didn't she might explode all over the place, or him.

"Do you want a glass of water?" Becca avoided looking at him by turning to go to the cabinet where the glasses were kept.

"Yes, please." There was a trace of hidden laughter in his tone.

"Why are you here anyway?"

"Why else—to check on you."

The simmer was quickly turning into flaring temper. "Have a seat," she said with false calm. Back in Philadelphia, she thought, rather nastily.

Lunch was hardly a pleasant chatty occasion. In fact it was eaten in absolute silence.

Out of pure contrariness, not thirst, Becca drank two cups of the fresh coffee, while simply nibbling at both her salad and sandwich.

Naturally, Seth serenely ignored her while eating every bit of his lunch…not to mention the half of sandwich she left on her plate.

To Becca's further annoyance, he monitored every swallow of coffee she took.

"You know," he said, too casually, "instead of gulping caffeine, you should be resting."

Skirting the edge of serious anger, Becca glanced at him balefully. "Is that a professional or merely personal opinion, Dr. Andrews?"

He appeared unfazed by both her expression and sour tone of voice. "Both."

"Well, you can take both opinions and jam—"

"Careful now, Rebecca," he cautioned. "Let's not get down and dirty here."

Throwing her hands into the air, rather than her fist at his head, Becca shoved back her chair, stood and began clearing the table. "I don't want to listen to you issuing orders or suggestions." Carrying the dishes, she stopped halfway between the table and the sink to turn and face him. "You are not my boss here."

"I am not trying to boss you around." Seth shoved his chair back and circled the table to stand over her. Anger was beginning to color his voice. "Can't you see I'm trying to help you?"

"No." She gave a sharp shake of her head. "All I see is a man trying to tell me what to do and when to do it. Well, I'm tired of it." Becca drew a quick breath, and ranted on, "I have been telling you I am fine. Why can't you let it go at that?"

"Because you obviously aren't *fine*," he snapped back at her. "If you were *fine* you wouldn't have damn near collapsed in John's office."

Although Becca was well aware that everything he was saying was true, she couldn't admit it.

"Why don't you just go get your bag and go back to Philadelphia, and leave me alone?" She spun to go to the sink and deposit the dishes. "You're not my keeper, you're a surgeon. Go back and save someone's life, for heaven's sake!" She turned again, away from him. Gently but firmly grasping her by the upper arm, he stopped her in her tracks.

"The way you've been pushing yourself, you need a keeper." His voice had a ragged edge. Turning to face her, he clasped her other arm. "It might as well be me."

"I don't think so," Becca retorted, a shiver rippling through her when he raised his hand to cradle her face. "You're the last person…"

"Oh, Becca, shut up." With that, he very effectively shut her up himself, by covering her mouth with his.

Six

At first his kiss was really not a kiss at all, simply his cool lips on hers. Becca went stiff, ice invading her spine, freezing her to the spot with outrage.

Damned if he wasn't doing it to her again, kissing her to keep her quiet. *Oh, Becca, shut up.* Only this time he didn't press his mouth to hers almost as if he wanted to devour her.

And then, all hell broke loose inside her mind, her emotions, her entire body.

Seth's lips grew warm, his mouth taking command of hers as though it was his right, as though she belonged to him, was his to do with as he pleased.

She wanted to shove him away, but at that moment he slipped his hands from her face to wrap his arms around her, drawing her hard against him.

She lifted her hands to scratch at his face, tangled her fingers in his hair to tear at it, pull it from his scalp.

Her rioting emotions, frustration, need, emptiness and a sudden flare of physical response stilled her hands, turning her fury into passion.

She did slide her fingers into his hair, but to tug his head closer. His tongue swept inside her mouth, teased her tongue, sending electrical shock waves throughout her body. The tips of her breasts tightened and tingled all the way down to her feminine core. Without thought or direction, Becca arched into him.

He made a low, almost growling sound in his throat, thrust his tongue deep inside. Tightening his arms around her, he trailed one hand to the base of her spine, crushing her to the hard readiness of his body.

She felt him…all the way from the top of her head to the tip of her now tingling toes. Somewhere, in the very back of what was left of her mind, Becca thought she should stop him.

No, no, she banished the dimming thought. She didn't want to stop him, she wanted… Releasing her fingers from his silky hair, she curled her arms around his neck and hung on, hungrily returning the kiss as if her life depended on it.

With an urgent need to breathe, Seth again lifted

his head. Becca wanted to protest, but she couldn't speak. He didn't loosen his hold on her and she continued to cling to him. Resting her forehead against his heaving chest, she shivered to the excited arousal racing along her nervous system, tangoing up her spine.

"Ahhh, Becca." Raising her chin with his other hand, he again lowered his head to command her mouth with his.

This time his kiss was gentle, teasing, his tongue playing hide-and-seek with hers. Kissed senseless, beyond coherent thought, she simply melted into him, returning the kiss, joining with his playful tongue.

She was only vaguely aware of being lifted into his arms. His increasingly hungry mouth setting her on fire, she clung to him as he strode into her bedroom, kicking the door shut behind them.

"Seth…" she began, only to have him silence her with one finger over her lips.

"Now is not the time for talk, Becca," he murmured, gliding his finger over her bottom lip. "Now is the time for indulgence, of our senses, in each other."

A tremor of longing rippled through her at the images his words evoked. Images right out of her dreams about him, them, together. Without a murmur of protest, Becca raised her mouth to his.

Within minutes, without breaking the kiss, they

slipped out of their clothing. Then finally, skin to skin, they fell onto the bed together.

Seth's body was hot and smooth and hard. She shivered in the heat of him. She trembled as his hands began to move, caressing her body.

A soft protest sprang to her throat when his mouth left hers. Her protest swiftly changed to a moan as his lips tracked the path of his hands.

Following his lead, Becca skimmed her hands over every inch of his body she could reach. She loved the feel of his hot skin beneath her palms. His back was broad, muscles taut with expectation. She traced the length of his spine. Emboldened by the quiver of his body, she smoothed her hands over his tight, narrow buttocks then stretched to slide her palms down his muscled bunched thighs. He made a guttural sound deep in his throat as she skimmed her fingers up the insides of his thighs.

Her own muffled groan echoed his as his one hand cupped one of her bottom cheeks and the other hand cupped her mound.

Without conscious thought, her thighs parted. She gasped with surprised pleasure when his fingers found and teased the most sensitive spot on her body.

"Seth…" That was all she could manage to say between short harsh breaths.

"You like that?" His voice was low, pure temptation. His mouth sought and found her breast, lips closing around the tip.

This time she couldn't manage even one word. But her gasp, the tremor that cascaded down her body, told him all he needed to know. "You like that, too?" His warm breath bathed her wet nipple, causing her to shiver.

Becca was long past denial. "Yes, yes, yes," she said, raking her nails down his back.

"Umm…" he murmured, shivering in response. "And I like that." Sliding up over her, he took her mouth in a soul-stirring, mind-destroying kiss. "And I like that." He deepened the kiss. "And that," he whispered against her lips before drawing a shudder from her by gliding his tongue along the inside of her lower lip. "But I like what's next even more." Kneeing her thighs wider, he settled between them.

She half expected to suddenly wake up, as she always did in her dreams when he slid between her thighs.

But Becca knew she wasn't dreaming when with one thrust he was inside her, filling the aching emptiness.

This was Seth inside her, pleasuring her, driving her higher and higher. It was wonderful. Aroused beyond anything she would ever have imagined herself to be capable of, Becca went wild in response.

Her breathing harsh, her body growing moist with perspiration, she arched up, into his every thrust, wanting more and more of him.

Leaning down over her, his hands covered her breasts as his lips covered her mouth, his tongue thrusting in rhythm with his body.

Becca was certain she was dying, or would if the tension, the friction of their joining, went on much longer. "I…I…" She gulped a breath. "Seth, please, I can't…I can't take any more."

"Do you want me to stop?" His voice was a purr that stroked her senses, incited her hunger.

"No!"

"Then, what do you want?" He had slowed his rhythm. "Tell me, Becca."

"You know." She grasped him by the hips, urging him deeper, deeper. "You know what I want."

"Yes," he whispered, plunging hard and fast. "I know, because I want it, too."

Becca went frantic as the tension built higher… higher…and then it snapped, flinging her wildly into a place she had never been. She cried out with the joy of it.

The very next instant, as if from a far distance, she heard Seth grunt before crying out his own release from the shatteringly wonderful tension.

Collapsing on top of her, Seth buried her face in the curve of her neck. Bearing his weight, Becca cradled him in an embrace of her arms and legs as their labored breathing slowly returned to normal.

Satiated, completely fulfilled and wonderfully drained, Becca closed her eyes, beginning to drift in the area between wakefulness and sleep.

She felt Seth move, shift his body from hers to lie next to her on the bed. She shivered and Seth drew her to him, while pulling the comforter over both of them.

Sighing with the double sensations of warmth and safety, Becca surrendered to slumber.

It was dark when Becca stirred to the delightful sensations created by Seth's hands stroking her now sensitized skin. Barely awake, her body responded to the arousing glide of his hand as it skimmed from her hip to her breasts, caressing one and then the other.

She sighed as his mouth moved over her face, leaving tiny kisses in its wake. She moaned with need when his lips took hers and his free hand delved into the apex of her legs, testing her readiness. Clasping him to her, she returned his kiss, her mouth and body demanding more, more of the ecstasy he had already given her.

With a soft chuckle, Seth obeyed, sliding his body between her parted thighs.

This time there was no teasing play. There was just a mutual urgency driving them. Seth was demanding, and so was Becca. She wanted to wring every drop of passion from him.

Seth didn't disappoint her. His thrusting body drove her quickly to the edge and over it. Becca's near scream of exquisite satisfaction and delicious pleasure was silenced inside his mouth.

She felt as if she had died, and didn't care. Close to unconsciousness, she was barely aware of Seth's tortured breath as he muttered close to her ear.

"That was fantastic."

They were the last words she heard before falling into a deep sleep.

Becca woke alone in the bed. Before opening her eyes, she floated in her dreams. They were like all the others, except this time she hadn't awakened at the most crucial moment. A soft smile on her lips, she opened her eyes, blinking at the bright sunlight streaming through the two bedroom windows.

What time was it? she wondered, yawning and glancing at the beside clock. *After ten? When had she gone to bed?* Her mind still a little hazy, she tossed back the comforter. The ache in her inner thighs, the tenderness in the apex of her legs, brought consciousness and memory flooding her mind.

Seth.

Turning her head, Becca looked at the empty space next to her. She sniffed, then drew a deep breath. She could smell him, the combined odors of sex and sweat and Seth's own masculine scent.

Memories continued to play inside her mind. His kisses, his caresses, his...*twice!* It was all there, in full color. Becca grew warm with a flush spreading from her cheeks to the rest of her body. She felt hot again and needy and...something niggled at the fringes of her mind, something important that she couldn't grasp.

She needed a shower. Not a cold one like men needed to ward off building passion, but a hot one that always left her feeling limp and drowsy.

Moving slowly, grimacing at the pull in her legs, Becca sat up onto the edge of the bed, tentatively getting to her feet. Okay, so far. Standing, she slowly walked into the bathroom. After standing under the hot spray from the shower for several minutes, she emerged, the flush of desire gone, along with much of the stiffness in her legs, the tenderness between them.

Becca stood in the steamy bathroom, blow-drying her hair, when the niggling sensation in her mind burst forth with its revelation. The echo of Seth's murmured words as she had drifted off to sleep came through loud and clear.

That was fantastic.

Meaning fantastic sex. That's all he'd thought it was. Just sex. A chill washed over her, chasing the warmth from the shower, leaving her body shivering. Biting her lip to hold back threatening tears, Becca turned off the dryer and rushed into the bedroom to dress.

Damn him, she raged in furious silence. He had done it again. Only this time, instead of being satisfied with merely shutting her up with a kiss, he had taken it to the limit, using her to satisfy himself with her body. And she, blind fool that she was, had surrendered herself to him.

How could she ever face him again? What must he be thinking of her? She had been eager, wanton, a willing partner in his self-indulgence.

That Seth had given her unimaginable pleasure in return didn't matter. Becca now knew she was not just infatuated with him. She was in love with him, while he...he...

Sniffing, she finished fastening her bra, swiped a hand over her moist eyes and pulled a hot pink T-shirt over her head. Telling herself she absolutely refused to cry over any man, she sniffed again while stepping into jeans, noting that although they were still loose on her, they weren't as loose as they had been two weeks ago.

Slipping into ballerina flats, Becca glanced into the mirror, grimacing at the wild tangled mess of her dark, straight hair. As she tamed her hair with a brush, she caught the aroma of brewing coffee and frying bacon. Sue must be back and cooking break-fast…and it smelled wonderful.

Her stomach rumbled. The eyes reflected back at her from the mirror widened. How could she be hungry at a time like this? Becca frowned at her re-flection. Maybe because she hadn't eaten since she had picked at her lunch yesterday. Not to mention the "exercise" in the afternoon and during the night.

But Becca didn't want to think about that. Satis-fied with just smoothing moisturizer on her face, she skipped makeup and left the room.

Maybe, just maybe, if she were lucky, Becca thought as she made her way to the kitchen, after what happened between them, Seth had left the house earlier and was on his way back to Philadelphia.

She should live so long.

Becca took one step inside the kitchen and stopped dead in her tracks. Sue was not in the room. Instead, Seth stood at the stove, pouring beaten eggs from a bowl into a sizzling frying pan. He glanced over his shoulder at her, saw her cool expression and raised his brows.

"Good morning." He didn't smile.

"Morning." She didn't smile, either.

He did frown. "Have a seat, breakfast will be ready in a few minutes." He turned away to stir the eggs and flip over the bacon.

Ignoring his invitation, Becca walked to the coffeepot and filled one of the mugs set on the countertop. Then she returned to sit down at the table. Carefully sipping the hot brew, she watched him lay pieces of bacon onto a towel to drain, then separate the eggs onto two plates. He was doing the same with the bacon when she spoke.

"I'm not very hungry." Her stomach clutched at the bald-faced lie.

Now, Seth ignored her. He brought the two plates to the table and set one in front of her. "You must be," he said mildly. "You haven't eaten anything but those couple of bites of your sandwich yesterday."

"But—" she began, only to have him cut in.

"Eat, Becca," he ordered. "Or do you want to make yourself ill all over again?"

"Of course not," she protested, her mouth watering from the scent of the eggs and bacon wafting to her. "I'm just—"

"You're just what?" Sharp impatience rode his tone. "Waiting for the toast? It's on a plate right there in the middle of the table."

"But…" she tried again, to no avail.

Seth scowled at her, and said coldly, "Becca, shut up and eat."

Shut up…again? She glared at him.

He glared right back at her. Then he shrugged. "Have it your own way. I'm hungry and the food's getting cold." Looking away from her, he calmly began to eat.

For a moment, her mind and her stomach battled. When he reached for a piece of toast and slathered strawberry jam on it, her stomach won. With a soft sigh of defeat, Becca dug in to her breakfast.

They ate in tense, uneasy silence. Even so, Becca finished every morsel on her plate and two pieces of toast. She moved to get up to refill her mug. Seth was faster. Rising, he walked to the countertop and brought the pot back to the table with him. After filling both mugs, he set the pot down and turned to look at her.

"Okay, what's your problem?" he said, continuing before she could think of a response. "Regret? Remorse? Shame? Guilt?"

She held his steady gaze while corralling her thoughts into a cohesive reply.

"All of the above?" he asked.

"No. Yes." Becca shook her head at the demanding note in his voice. "I don't know."

Seth gave a deep sigh. "Becca, I don't understand. This morning you give me the cold shoulder. After last night I thought—"

"Yes, I know what you thought," she snapped back at him. "You thought it was great sex."

"No," he denied. "I thought it was fantastic sex. So, what's wrong with that?"

What was wrong with that? Becca asked herself, raking her mind for an answer. Well, in all honesty, nothing was wrong with fantastic sex. In fact, fantastic sex was…well, fantastic…between two committed people. But they—she and Seth—weren't committed. She now realized she was in love with him, crazy in love with him. So then, wasn't she committed?

Maybe she ought to be committed, into a room with padded walls, she chided herself.

"So?" Seth prompted her after her lengthy silence. "I asked what's wrong with that?"

"I…" She shook her head, shrugged, desperate for a coherent response. "I don't…" She was interrupted by the kitchen door swinging open, Sue practically dancing into the room.

"Good morning," she said, her voice light with a happy note.

Becca's immediate thought was that it would appear Sue had enjoyed some pretty good sex, as well. "Good morning, Sue." She and Seth spoke in unison. Relieved at being saved from answering him, she asked, "Have you had breakfast?"

"Yes." Pink tinged her cheeks. "John and I had the breakfast buffet at the Coffee Shop."

"This Coffee Shop does breakfast buffet?" Seth arched his brows. "Every morning?"

Sue shook her head. "No, only on the weekend.

They lay it on, too. The place gets packed." The color deepened in her cheeks. "John made reservations last night to make sure we could get in."

"Hmm, I'll keep that in mind." He shifted a glance at Becca. "Where is this place located?"

"Halfway down the street from John's office." Sue flushed again, obviously with the mere mention of John's name. "Is there any coffee?" she asked, neatly changing the conversation.

"It's gone cold." Becca slid her chair back. "I'll make a fresh pot."

Seth's chair scraped back at the same time. "No, I'll make it."

Becca stood and favored him with a patently fake smile. "You can clear the table. I'll get the coffee." She turned her attention to Sue before he could utter a protest. "So, how was your dinner?"

"It was wonderful, John cooked it." The flush was back. "How was the chicken veggie pie?"

Pie? Becca stopped cold, her mind a momentary blank. Memory returned, and her cheeks flushed. Oh, heavens, the supper Sue had prepared for them. They had completely forgotten, with good reason. She flashed a quick look at Seth. A tiny smile played at the corners of his lips, and arching a brow, he blandly returned her look.

No help from that quarter. Facing Sue, she plastered a smile on her lips. "I'm afraid I never got to it. I made do with lunch, then went right to my room." She shot Seth a smug look and an innocent tone. "What about you, Seth. Did you have the pie for dinner?"

"No, I didn't want to bake it just for myself," he returned, his voice smooth, unruffled. "I didn't have much of an appetite anyway." He gave Sue a charming, disarming smile. "The three of us can have it for dinner tonight, if you're planning on being here."

"Oh, I am, but—" Sue hesitated, before looking at Becca and rushing on "—I hope you don't mind, Becca, I've invited John to dinner. I'm sure there'll be enough pie for the four of us."

"Of course, I don't mind," Becca said, silently sighing with relief. Hopefully, the tension between her and Seth would dry up with Sue and John there. "As for being enough, we can always add to the salad Seth and I didn't finish yesterday."

"Oh, thank you." Sue sighed aloud. "I know I should have asked you first but..."

"Don't be silly," Becca said, bringing the coffee-pot and a clean mug to the table. "Coffee's ready. Do you want a refill, Seth?"

"Yes, thank you," he eyed her warily, as if not sure from her pleasant tone what her mood was.

"Well, I've had enough coffee this morning. I think I'll collect my laundry and wash it." Despite

Sue's arguments, Becca had insisted from the day after she arrived at the house that she would do her own wash. She was walking through the archway into the dining room when she leveled a zinger at Seth over her shoulder. "I think I'll launder the sheets, as well."

"But I thought you just changed sheets three days ago," Sue called after her.

Becca halted, a wicked smile feathering her lips. "I did, but I had a couple of nightmares last night, and I was perspiring all over the sheets. They now have a bad smell."

Seven

"Sweaty and smelly from nightmares, are they?"

Becca froze at the sound of Seth's low-pitched voice. Her fingers curled into the bottom sheet she had been tugging from the mattress.

"Strange…they didn't seem like nightmares to me. They were a lot more pleasurable than nightmares."

Oh, why had she left her bedroom door open? she wondered, afraid Sue might be able to hear him. Bracing herself, she turned to face him. He was standing at the doorway. He hadn't taken one step inside.

"May I come in?" Seth's smile was wry. "Even though it's mighty tempting with those sheets all rumpled and smelling of sex, I promise I won't pick you up and toss you onto the bed."

Damn right you won't, Becca thought. "I didn't suspect you would," she said.

His brows went up. "Then…?"

"Why, what do you want?"

Now the smile that crept over his alluring mouth, the sudden darkening of his amber eyes, said volumes without him uttering a sound. "I think we need to talk."

"All right, come in." She sighed. "But…" There was a warning note in her voice.

"You have my word," he murmured, stepping inside and quietly closing the door behind him.

"Okay, talk away," Becca said, turning back to continue stripping the bed.

Unfazed, he circled the bed to the padded boudoir chair set next to the window. "May I?" He indicated the small chair.

Becca didn't look away from what she was doing, only yanked harder on the sheets. "If you must," she said, sighing loudly.

He chuckled softly, seating himself.

His laughter tickled down the length of her spine and back up to the nape of her neck. Why did the man have such a melting effect on her? He always had, and Becca had worked hard all the years she'd assisted him not to betray her feelings.

Watching him with quick sidelong glances as she worked, she saw him stretch his long legs out and cross his ankles. While she mused that by rights he should look uncomfortable in the small chair, he managed to appear completely relaxed.

How did he do that? Puzzled by his apparent comfort in the lady's chair, Becca slid another long glance at him and immediately wished she hadn't, for he was watching her.

"You said you wanted to talk." Irritation, more at herself than him, shaded her tones. "About what?"

"First, I'd like to know why you had to mention anything to Sue about having to change the sheets? I was thinking we had a great time making those sheets sweaty and smelly. But then, I had believed you were thinking the same."

Her mind a sudden blank, Becca stood there by the bed staring at him, the soiled linens bundled in her arms.

Of course, she knew the answer. She'd said it because she felt hurt, used and longing for something more than sex. She loved him. She wanted nothing more than to repeat their night together every night for the rest of her life.

But Seth didn't love her. It didn't take a genius to figure that one out. Oh, she supposed he liked her okay, in his own gruff way, and certainly he respected her ability as his assistant in the operating room. But he had never once indicated any personal interest in her before. So why now, and here?

Suddenly she realized she had been quiet too long, simply staring into his now closed expression. What had he said? Oh, yeah, something about him believing she'd enjoyed their lovemaking as much as he had.

"I admit I did enjoy our night together," she finally replied. "It had…uh, been a while for me," she blurted out, at once regretting the admission.

His expression went from closed to hard and cold. "I see…I was a handy convenience." His voice was every bit as hard and cold as his expression.

Becca felt almost as though he had slapped her. Without a thought, she retaliated. "It appears we were handy conveniences for each other."

"Umm." That was the only sound he made. Slowly, his gaze still locked onto hers, his expression softened, his eyes warmed with sensuality. "In that case, while I'm here, why not continue the arrangement?" A half smile formed on his lips. "Sex is a healthy outlet for tension and stress, and we've both endured plenty of that for some time."

Stunned speechless, Becca simply stared at him, unable to believe he had actually said that to her. But then, he was a man and she'd read somewhere that men thought about sex every few minutes. Seth had very likely been celibate for a long time. At least she felt sure he hadn't been with a woman during the time he had been in Africa. As small as the village was, the grapevine was always up and running and she'd have heard about it if he had been seeing a woman.

Of course, Seth had been back in Philadelphia for a month now. He could have... Becca didn't want to think about what he could have been doing.

"I hate to intrude on your introspection, but is your silence a way of saying no to my proposal?" Now his voice was bone-dry, and a little gravelly.

Becca felt stuck between a rock of pride and a hard place of desire. Which did she need more, her pride or...? Pride lost the battle hands down.

"How long are you planning on being here?" she asked, avoiding giving him a definite answer.

"I told Colin I'd be gone a week." He shrugged. "Colin has held it together long enough. It's time I got back to work."

"I like Colin," Becca said, fully aware she was biding for extra time.

"So do I or I wouldn't be in practice with him," he said, giving a brief shake of his head. "But that has nothing to do with the subject at hand. All I want, Becca, is a yes or a no."

She drew a breath, a deep one, once again avoiding an answer by saying, "I'll think about it and let you know." What a coward you are, Becca derided herself. Too gutless to grab what you want.

"Your call," Seth said, rising to nonchalantly stroll to the door, where he paused to glance back at her. "While you're thinking, keep in mind that we're both adults," he said. "At least, I am." He walked out, closing the door quietly behind him.

"Damn," Becca muttered, flinging the bundle of sheets to the floor. She stood still for a moment, breathing hard. He was right. He was an adult. She was the one acting like a child…a bad-tempered one at that.

She opened a dresser drawer to take out a set of clean sheets and proceeded to remake the bed.

As she hadn't eaten breakfast until late morning, Becca skipped lunch and spent the rest of the afternoon in her room, relaxing and reading, but in plain truth, she was hiding from Seth.

In an attempt to keep her thoughts at bay, she took a long, hot bath, scrubbing every inch of her body with a single-mindedness that left her skin tingling.

By the time Becca had done her hair and was dressed in wide-legged flowing pants and a loose pullover top, she had made up her mind as to exactly what her answer to Seth was going to be.

Finally leaving her bedroom, Becca's steps were light as she walked into the kitchen. Sue was bent over, her head stuck in the fridge.

"Are you caught in there, Sue?" she said, laughing as she crossed to the older woman. "Can I help?"

Laughing along with her, Sue backed out of the fridge, the chicken vegetable pie in her hands. "Yes, you can get the salad and cut up more ingredients to toss into it to stretch it to make enough for four." She raised her eyebrows. "You did remember that John is coming for dinner?"

"Yes, I remembered." Becca took Sue's place in the fridge, gathering veggies from the bottom drawer. "What time do you expect him?" she asked, straightening and shutting the door with a swing of her hips.

Sue was sliding the pie into the oven. "I told him six," she said, closing the oven door. "Did you have a nice nap?"

"Not really." Becca grinned. "I guess I wasn't as tired as I thought." She glanced around and into the dining room and the living room beyond. "Where is Seth?"

"John invited him into town for the grand tour, which shouldn't take very long." Sue smiled. "I suppose they're in the clinic and he and Seth are having a gabfest." She glanced at the clock. "It's five now." Her smile turned into a laugh. "I suspect they'll be here in time for dinner."

"They'd better be," Becca said, holding a strainer under running water, rinsing the grape tomatoes inside the bowl. "This is going to be one hummer of a salad."

* * *

It was a fine September Sunday afternoon, the perfect weather for a stroll around the town of Forest Hills. After making the circuit, John invited Seth back to the clinic for a cup of coffee and some conversation.

Seth sat in the chair beside John's desk. They were sipping John's strong coffee, getting to know one another, biding time until they were due to return to the house for dinner.

"You know, I've heard of your father," John said out of the blue. "It's said he's one of the best heart surgeons in the world."

"You heard correctly." Seth smiled. "In the operating room, my father's a power to be reckoned with. He beats the odds more often than he loses."

"I heard about you, too." John smiled at him. "You started up the hospital in Africa your father and a few other doctors built."

"Correct again." Seth laughed. "I presume you heard of me because of all the attention Becca received when I sent her back to the States."

John shook his head. "Oh, yes, I couldn't have missed that as it was all over the news. But I had heard of you before, in connection to the hospital, as well as the reputation you've built in your own field of expertise."

Seth shrugged off the praise, addressing only his

work in Africa. "I didn't do anything spectacular. A doctor was needed in that village and I offered to go. No big deal."

"You did nothing spectacular except bring much-needed hope and medical care to those people in that town," John said.

"Yeah, but my dad and his friends made it all possible by financing the hospital," Seth said. "Becca's the heroine of that story."

John nodded in agreement. "From what I read, she gave her all to those people and her profession."

For a moment, Seth felt a twinge of the familiar fear. "She damn near killed herself." His quavering voice betrayed his feelings. He cleared his throat and said, "And even so, she argued about leaving."

"You like her, don't you?" John said, obviously noting the concern hiding behind his rough tone.

"Yes, of course," Seth answered, thinking, no, *like* didn't even come close to the depth of what he felt for Becca. It was a feeling he wasn't about to confess to John, or anyone except Becca—maybe.

"She has been a great help to me here since she arrived," John said. "After she leaves, I'll be back on my own...unless I can talk Sue into taking Becca's place. Sue is a nurse, you know."

Seth shook his head, frowning. "I don't...wait a minute. The letter Becca received did mention that Sue was a nurse. I suppose I thought she had retired from nursing, and was supplementing her income by being the housekeeper for the person who owns that lodge they dare call a cabin."

John laughed. "Yeah, some cabin, huh?" Still chuckling, he clarified, "Sue had retired from nursing to come home here to take care of her mother after her father passed away." He sighed. "She had been helping me out in the clinic now and then before she was offered the job of housekeeping the cabin, keeping it neat part-time between visitors and full-time while someone was there and…at a salary you wouldn't believe."

Seth grinned. "Yeah, I would. Whoever this person is who owns the place has to be a multimillionaire or even a billionaire. That dump is something." He chose not to mention that his own father had a place that put the so-called cabin to shame.

John grinned back at him, and said in a soft, conspiratorial voice, "I have spent a few nights there with Sue when nobody was in residence."

Seth laughed, both at John's naughty-boy tone, and in a bid to conceal the shudder rippling through him at the vivid image of he and Becca sharing that big bed in the master bedroom.

Seth felt the stirring in his lower body. If he got hard now, John would think he was as horny as a teenager. Instead, John saved Seth's pride by glancing at his watch.

"We'd better be going," he said, standing. "Sue said six and it's ten of now. She won't like having to hold dinner. Besides, I'm hungry." Striding to the door, he opened it for Seth.

Seth was thinking he was hungry, too, but for Becca. His body calming down somewhat, he strolled from the room and the clinic to his car, which was parked right behind John's ten-year-old vehicle.

Food first, Seth thought, then…Becca's answer. He could only hope it would be the one he wanted to hear.

Sliding the tray of dinner rolls into the oven, Sue set the timer then glanced at the clock. "They had better get here soon," she muttered.

Becca glanced up to smile at the frowning woman. "There's time, it's only ten minutes till six," she said, glancing back at the table to make sure she hadn't missed anything.

As Sue had decided to eat dinner in the kitchen instead of at the much larger and formal dining room, Becca had set the table with the everyday dishes, the ones she and Sue had used ever since Becca had arrived.

Everything was ready. The white wine was chilling. Becca had uncorked the red to allow it to breathe. The large salad bowl was set to one side, four smaller matching bowls next to it. A selection of dressings sat behind the grouping of salt-and-pepper shakers and a crystal butter dish.

Satisfied, Becca went to the counter to shake out and place a napkin inside a basket for the rolls. She looked up, her heart beginning to race as the doors of two separate cars were slammed shut. Moments later came the sound of footsteps up and onto the porch.

She turned as the kitchen door was opened, repressing a shiver as the men entered the room. The shiver grew, chilling her spine as Seth's eyes immediately sought her out with a heated amber stare.

"We're back," John announced, voicing the obvious. "And with a few minutes to spare till six."

"You two can go wash up," Sue said, a warm smile on her lips for John. "Dinner is ready."

"Yes, ma'am," John said, his smile as warm as hers had been. "Let's go, Seth."

"Yes, sir," Seth replied, shooting a grin at Becca. "I'm right behind you."

His grin, both amused and intimate, played tricks with Becca's senses. Heat flared in the deepest part of her body. She was at once uncertain of the decision she had made about the answer she planned to give him. When a mere grin was all a man had to do to turn her on…well… The men's return to the kitchen scattered her already tumbling thoughts.

"Ahhh," John murmured, inhaling deeply. "That smells wonderful, Sue."

The Sue that Becca had come to know had seemed unflappable, but one minor compliment from the good doctor did the trick. Flushing, Sue set the large pie on the table and with a breathy "thanks" quickly turned to the stove to slide the tray of rolls from the oven.

Smiling in sympathy for the older woman, as Becca was still feeling a bit breathless herself, she retrieved the salad from the fridge. While Sue took a carafe of water from the fridge, Becca got the wine bottles and set them on the table.

To her surprise, the men waited to seat them before seating themselves. Becca assumed Seth had followed John's lead, as he had never held a chair for her in all the years she had worked for him, and they had taken lunch and dinner together many times before.

The meal was wonderful, the conversational topics all over the place. Sometimes serious, more often amusing, they lingered over their coffee and the apple pie Sue warmed in the oven before plopping big slabs of vanilla ice cream on top of each large slice.

By the time they made a move, seemingly as of one mind to leave the table, it was nearly seven forty-five. Becca felt about to burst, but she also felt mellow from the delicious food, the wine and the sense of camaraderie and contentment.

Both men began to collect the dishes. Sue put an end to their efforts to help.

"Becca and I'll do the clearing away," she said, making a shooing motion with her hands. "You two go watch the news or a football game or something."

"But you and Becca had the work of prepar—" That's as far as she allowed John to go.

"And Becca and I will clear it away. Now go," she ordered. "The sooner we get started, the sooner we'll get finished."

Neither Becca nor Seth said a word. They just stood by, smiling and watching. Well, Becca was smiling and watching Sue and John, but the sensation of the raised hairs on her arms, the tingle at the back of her neck, made her feel certain Seth was watching her. But while she felt as though she could feel his intent gaze on her, there was no way she could discern if he were smiling or frowning at her.

It was not a comfortable sensation. While doing her best to appear unaware of his stare, Becca lost track of the tug-of-war between Sue and John. She caught up with it just as John threw in the towel.

"Okay, okay, we'll go into the living room." John raised his hands in defeat. "Come on, Seth, let's get out of here before this comes to blows."

"As if," Sue retorted, laughing.

John and Seth sauntered from the room. Becca exhaled in relief, glad to be out from under the microscope of Seth's speculative gaze.

Starting to clear the table, she gave Sue a curious look. "Why were you so insistent on the men not pitching in to help out in here?"

"Because I wanted a minute to talk to you in private," Sue answered, her cheeks growing pink again. She carried a load of dishes to the dishwasher.

"Okay," Becca said, following her with the knives, forks and spoons. "About what?"

Sue straightened up from the dishwasher. "Becca, you're a nurse and a mature woman, and I hope you'll understand..." She trailed off, then burst out, "Oh, hell, Becca, I've asked John to stay over at my house tonight." She grabbed a breath. "Will you be all right alone here again tonight?"

Now Becca did laugh, gently. "Of course I'll be all right. And I won't be alone, you know, Seth will be here with me."

Hearing her own words squelched her laughter. She quivered inside, remembering how they had spent the night, and his proposal.

"Whew," Sue said, beaming at Becca. "You'd figured out where I had spent last night, hadn't you?"

Becca lips quirked in a half smile. "Well, I had my suspicions."

"Oh, Becca, I have been in love with John for as long as I can remember." Noting Becca's quick frown, she hurried on. "Oh, don't misunderstand, I loved my husband dearly, but a tiny piece of my heart always belonged to John. And now…" Tears misted her eyes.

"Now he has discovered you?"

"Yes." Sue sniffed, followed by an uncertain smile. "We're both in our fifties and we don't want to waste any more time. Does that make sense to you?"

"That makes perfect sense, Sue." Becca smiled. "How did that old line go…something about only going around once?"

"Yes." Sue laughed. "You're right, so let's get done so John and I can get out of here."

It required less than twenty minutes to put the kitchen back in order. Appearing casual, Becca and Sue joined the men in the living room. They were watching a football game on TV.

Seth glanced up at Becca, a wry smile on his lips. "The Eagles are playing the Giants."

"Oh, that's nice." She didn't give a rip about football, and Seth knew it. "I think I'll get a book to read." She started for her room, but turned back to give Sue a pointed look. "Did you say something about you and John going out for a while, Sue?"

"Yes, I did." Sue returned the smile. "Are you about ready to go, John?"

"Whenever you are," he said, pushing out of the chair's deep cushions. "I'm a baseball fan myself."

Seth moved to rise.

"You don't need to get up, Seth," John said, offering him a man-to-man grin. "We know our way out."

"Well, 'bye now," Sue called, leading John by the arm to the door.

Seth stared at the doorway with a "what did I miss?" expression. Stifling a laugh, Becca turned again to go for a book. But she couldn't resist a mild teasing jab.

"You're missing the game." Before he could turn to her, she took off down the hallway to her room.

Seth was right behind her.

Although she didn't hear him, she knew he was there. The tingle up her spine gave warning. Arching her eyebrows in question, she turned to look at him.

Once again he stood at the doorway, not entering without her permission, still wearing the slightly baffled look on his face.

"What was that all about in there?"

Not wanting him to see the smile flitting across her mouth, Becca turned away again, simply asking, "What was what all about?"

"That exchange there in the living room just now," he said, impatience riding his voice. "That byplay between Sue and John…and you, too?"

The smile escaping, she slanted a sidelong glance at him. Umm, he looked sooo good, she thought.

"They were being coy, Seth. Sue and John are going to spend the night together." She chuckled. "I suspect they did last night as well."

"Sounds good to me," he said, his voice low and much too seductive.

"I feel sure it would sound good to most men," she murmured, expecting an argument as she turned fully to face him once more. He didn't give her one.

"Have you reached a decision?" His voice was softer, his eyes wary.

Becca drew a deep breath. "Yes, I'll spend the rest of the week with you."

"Good," his voice held a soft sigh of relief. Stepping inside, he crossed to her, halting abruptly when she held one hand up, palm out.

"But not tonight."

His eyes narrowed and one brow lifted in skepticism. "You have a headache?"

Eight

Becca gave him a wry look. "No, I don't have a headache, Seth."

"Then—" he began.

"But I ache everywhere else in my body."

"Oh…" He frowned.

Becca could tell by the sudden chagrined look on his face that he understood she was sore from their sexual exercise through most of the night.

"Yes," she said, allowing him a small smile. "So tonight I just want to read my book a while then get a good night's sleep."

"Of course." Seth nodded, smiling sympathetically. "Will you bring your book into the living room, sit with me while I watch the game?"

"If you'll recall," she pointed out to him, "I said that's what I was going to do."

"Good." Turning, he walked away.

Shaking her head in bemusement, Becca picked up the historical romance paperback from the bedside stand and followed him into the living room.

Earlier, Seth had been sitting in the butter-soft leather lounge chair. Now, he was on the sofa. He patted the cushion next to him when she entered the room.

"Come, sit beside me," he invited, soft and low.

Becca arched her brows.

"I'll behave," he said, grinning, and again patting the cushion. "I promise."

"Weelll…" she said, dragging the word out. "If you promise to keep your promise." Becca grinned back at him, as she settled on the couch beside him.

"Hmm," he murmured, appearing sad. "Does behaving include no kisses or hugs?"

His teasing and downcast look were so far out of character, it was simply too much. Becca burst out laughing.

"Is that a yes or a no?" His attempt to look and sound stern was pathetic.

She laughed harder. "I never knew you could be fun to be with," she admitted.

Seth jerked back, one hand flying to his chest, as if he had been shot. "You wound me, woman. Are you insinuating last night with me wasn't fun?"

Still laughing at his antics, Becca covered her mouth with one hand and shook her head in the negative.

This time he managed a killer, sensual smile. "You are so sexy when you laugh, did you know that?"

"Sexy! Me? I am?" Becca was stunned. "I'm not at all sexy," she declared, so thrilled by the compliment, the words seemed to tumble out of her mouth. "At least, no one has ever given me the slightest hint they thought I was sexy."

"You're not serious…are you?" One dark eyebrow arched in disbelief.

"You think I'd kid around about something like that?" she said, a tinge of annoyance in her voice, a cover-up for her sense of inadequacy. She made a move to get up, put some distance between them.

"Whoa, you stay right where you are," Seth ordered, curving his arm around her waist. "Better yet, come here, closer to me." He drew her stiffened body against him, raising a hand to turn her face to his.

Becca tried to move her head. He held her still, staring deeply into her eyes.

"To me, Becca, you are the sexiest woman I've ever set eyes on." He moved closer, brushing his lips over her mouth.

Becca shivered in response and inched closer to him for more of the same. "Really?" she whispered, returning the favor by brushing her mouth over his lips.

"Hmm," he murmured. "I've been wanting to get you into my bed, be inside you, ever since you became a member of my surgical team."

Becca inwardly cringed against a pang in her chest. He wanted her, physically, nothing more. She closed her eyes against a rush of hot tears as Seth took possession of her mouth, and thrust his tongue between her teeth.

For a moment she went still in his arms, his kiss was physically thrilling and emotionally devastating. She wanted to push him away, but clutched him to her instead. He hadn't lied to her, but had honestly admitted he wanted an affair, a week together of sexual fun and games.

While she, like a romantic fool, loved him with everything inside her being.

Desperately needing to release the tears gathering in her eyes in a long self-pity party of weeping, Becca pushed gently against his chest.

Seth was frowning when he lifted his head to gaze at her in confusion. "What's wrong?"

"I did tell you not tonight, Seth," she said, wincing at the painful tug of her lower back and inner thigh muscles as she rose from the sofa. "Now things are getting too intense. Not only do I still ache all over, now my head is beginning to pound."

"Let me get you some Tylenol or something stronger," he said, rising to stand next to her, and sliding his arm around her waist. "You are a little pale."

"Tylenol will be fine, thank you." Unable to resist, she rested her now throbbing head on his shoulder. "I don't like to take stronger pain medication. I'm just tired. I'll be okay after a good night's sleep."

"I'm not so sure about that," he muttered. It was only then she felt his finger on her wrist. "Your pulse rate is rapid. Looks like you've managed to overdo it once again."

"No, the rapid pulse is your fault," she admitted, managing a tiny smile. "That's the effect your kisses have on me."

He smiled. "That's a good thing." He immediately grew sober again. "I'm going to get my stethoscope." He started to turn away.

"No," she said, catching him by the arm. "It's not necessary." She frowned. "You brought your stethoscope with you on vacation?"

"Habit." He grinned.

"Uh-huh." Becca sighed, knowing full well he had come for the express reason to check on her. That also would have been a good thing, if he hadn't bluntly told her he wanted her to get well because he needed her in the operating room.

She sighed again. While the tears in her eyes were now gone, she still felt the urge to cry. "I think I'll forget reading tonight and go on to bed."

"Maybe that's best," he agreed, peering at her in his patient probing way. "You go ahead, I'll get the Tylenol and a glass of water."

Seth sat sprawled on the sofa, staring blindly at the TV screen. He didn't see the game in play, or hear the noise of the crowd of football fans or the chatter of the commentators.

The fire in his body had finally calmed down. The concern for Becca remained, worrying him. He didn't understand. She had seemed fine last night in bed, so sweetly responsive, ready...no, eager to share her body with him. Shivering, he grew warm remembering the honey of her mouth, the tight peaks of her breasts, the satin softness of her skin, her smooth thighs curled tightly around his waist.

Seth heaved a long sigh. He wanted to be lying next to her right now, not for the sex, although that would be wonderful, too. Most of all, he wanted to hold her close to him, make her completely well, keep her warm and safe, protect her for the rest of his life.

But Becca had made it obvious, many times, if not by words but attitude, that she was impervious to him and, apparently, any man. She was and had always been cool, calm and remote.

Except last night.

Last night. Closing his eyes, Seth rested his head on the back of the sofa, reliving every minute of the night before, every kiss, every touch, every cry of release and heady satisfaction.

He had never experienced anything even close to the euphoria he had shared with Becca.

She had given him this week. One week of being together day and night. On the spot, Seth vowed to make it the best week of his, and hopefully Becca's, life.

Her head throbbing, Becca lay across the bed fully dressed, but did not immediately fall asleep, as she had hoped she would. Slowly, the Tylenol eased the pain in her head, but it didn't induce sleepiness. Her mind was restless, spinning from one thought to the next, always coming back to the most important of all her jumbled mental meanderings.

She wanted Seth so very badly…body, heart and soul. Having been with him, in the most physical, intimate ways a woman can be with a man, she felt bereft without him next to her, holding her, loving her.

Loving her.

A sob rose in Becca's throat. She swallowed hard, attempting to force it back. Instead, it broke from her lips. She buried her face in her pillow to muffle the painful sound.

Until recently, Becca rarely allowed herself the indulgence of tears. In her teens, she had concluded giving way to tears only ever got two results—puffy eyes and a pale, blotchy face. Who needed that?

She had cried with Shakana before leaving Africa, but that was because she was ill and weak. Now, Becca was no longer ill or weak, at least physically. Emotionally, she was a basket case.

And so she cried, sobbing into the pillow until there were no more tears left inside her. She felt empty and she found peace in the haven of deep sleep.

Hours later, Becca woke, feeling washed out and used up and cold. Her eyelids felt heavy and odd. She hadn't closed the drapes and the light from a nearly full moon filled the room. She could see clearly. What she saw confused her for a moment.

She was fully dressed lying on top of the covers. Becca frowned. What was she doing in bed in her clothes? She moved her head on the pillow, grimacing at the wet touching her cheek. Why was the pillow... Oh. Dawn broke, not beyond the window but inside her now fully awake mind.

She had soaked the pillow with her useless tears.

She no longer wondered why her eyes felt funny. Sighing, she dragged her body from the bed, made her way to the bathroom and flipped on the light.

The image that stared back at her from the mirror was not encouraging. Her eyes were red-rimmed, the lids swollen. Her complexion looked like it had developed a bad rash while she slept.

"This is what you get for allowing yourself to become involved with a man who wants nothing from you but casual sex, even if he is the most skilled and exciting lover and otherwise wonderful man you have ever met."

Somehow, berating herself aloud had little effect on the ravaged image before her. Shaking her head in despair of the pitiful-looking creature in the mirror, Becca turned the faucet on until the water running from it felt almost icy.

Soaking a washcloth, she held it against her face, applying pressure to her eyes. She repeated the process several times, until her face felt numb with cold. After patting her face dry, she glanced into the mirror once more. She was red as a beet, but the swelling in her eyelids was down.

Knowing the cold-induced color would fade, Becca returned to the bedroom and switched on the bedside lamp. The digital number on the clock read 4:11 a.m.

Becca was wide-awake, shivering with the cold,

and suddenly hungry. First things first, she thought. Pulling off her clothes, goose bumps rising on her skin from the chill air, she slipped on an equally chilled silky nightgown. Grateful to Rachael for packing her ankle-length velour robe, she shrugged into its warmth and tied the belt snugly around her waist.

Now…food, she thought, sliding her cold feet into fuzzy, flat mule slippers. Before leaving the room, Becca went to the window to place her hand against the pane. Uh, yep, the night had turned very cold. Why she was surprised, she didn't know. It was September, and hard as it was to believe, two months had passed since she had returned to the States from Africa.

Time flies when you're having fun, she mused, grimacing as she left the room. And even if you weren't having fun.

Becca stopped in her tracks as she entered the living room. Seth was lying half on and half off the sofa, as if he had fallen asleep sitting up and slid down flat with his legs hanging over the edge. He appeared sound asleep. Becca could see he was now wearing pajama pants and a well-worn University of Pennsylvania sweatshirt. His feet were bare.

Realizing he was probably cold, Becca quietly walked to the sofa and carefully lifted his long legs onto the sofa. Taking the faux fur throw from the back of the sofa, she covered him, tucking the throw around his cold feet. Seth didn't wake up. He grunted and snuggled into the throw. Smiling, she backed away, turned and walked to the kitchen.

Becca was sitting at the kitchen table, chewing on a piece of toast and cradling a hot cup of tea in her hands, when Seth strolled into the room, the throw draped over his shoulders like a cape.

She raised her eyebrows. "Did I wake you when I covered you?"

He shook his head and smiled. "No, the smell of the bread toasting woke me. Smells good."

"Help yourself," she invited. "The bread's on the countertop, and bring a cup if you want some tea. I made a full pot." A flick of her hand indicated the fat china pot set close to her on the table.

"Thanks, I think I will."

Becca continued to eat her toast as she watched him make his own. She was finishing the last bite when he seated himself opposite her, pulling the throw around him like a robe.

"Turned cold during the night," he said, biting into a piece of toast.

"Yes," she agreed. "I guess Indian summer is over. I'll have to turn on the heat tomorrow…later today," she said, correcting herself.

"Hmm." Seth nodded, eyeing the teapot. "That tea smells good, too."

Unwilling to play either employee or hostess,

she refilled her cup, then slid the pot to him so he could pour his own tea.

"Thanks," he drawled, taking another big bite of the bread. "Couldn't you sleep?"

"I did sleep," she said, raising the cup to sip the hot brew. "I fell asleep on top of the covers. The chilly air, along with a pang of hunger, woke me."

"Oh." Seth continued to eat.

Becca concentrated on her tea, unable to think of another thing to add to such scintillating conversation.

Finishing off the last of his toast, Seth concentrated on his own tea...for a few moments. "You look tired, Becca," he said, sounding more the lover than the doctor.

A tingle attacking her spine, Becca lowered her eyes, murmuring simply, "I am tired."

"Come to bed with me, Becca." His voice was low, seductive, so very tempting.

The tingle in her spine flared into a full-fledged sizzle. She raised her eyes to stare into the depths of molten amber. "I..." She hesitated.

"Please." An imploring note added inducement to his passion-roughened voice.

"Seth, I—"

"I promise I'll be gentle, careful of your sore, aching muscles."

She paused, sighed and gave in to the hunger clawing at her body. "Yes."

Seth stood, pushing the chair back, and started toward her, his arms reaching for her.

"Seth, wait." Becca help up a hand. "I've got to clear away our dishes."

He rolled his eyes, sighed in exasperation. "Becca, the dishes can wait," he said, plucking her plate from her hands before taking her in his arms. "I'm not so certain I can."

Becca didn't struggle.

He swept her up into his arms, and started for her bedroom. The throw fluttered to the floor unnoticed.

Curling her arms around his neck, Becca rested her head against his shoulder, inhaling the spicy scent of his cologne and the even spicier natural scent of Seth beneath.

Nine

Seth carried Becca into her bedroom. A light nudge of his hip shut the door after them.

Setting her on her feet, he opened the belt on her robe. It slid silently down to the floor. Stepping back, he ran a head-to-toe look over her. A smile touched his lips. "Cute slippers."

Becca smiled back. "They're warm and comfortable." Her smile grew. "And, yes, cute."

Seth ran another glace the length of her. "The slippers are cute," he repeated, his eyes heating as his smile faded. "The nightgown is lovely...but I prefer you in your glorious natural state."

"Seth..." His name was all Becca could get past

her suddenly dry-as-dust throat. Her pulse jumped when he grasped the edges of his sweatshirt and pulled it up and over his head. He stood there, naked except for the cotton pajama pants riding low on his slim hips.

Lifting her eyes to his, Becca held his gaze as she drew the nightgown straps over her shoulders, allowing the gown to slide down her body to pool around her feet.

Once more Seth ran a slow look over her body.

Becca stepped out of the slippers and into his arms. A tremor skipped through her at the feel of his hands outlining her form.

"You're still too thin," he murmured close to her ear. "I can feel your hip bones jutting out."

Becca sent her own hands exploring. "You're still thin yourself, Doctor," she whispered. "Your hip bones jut out as far as mine."

She could feel his smile as he glided his lips from her ear to the corner of her mouth. "Your skin is silky again," he said, laughter in his tone. He brushed his mouth over hers. "Your lips are sweet."

Becca speared her fingers through the thick strands of his hair. "It's the jam I had on my toast."

He laughed aloud. "Ah, Becca, never without a comeback." He taste-tested her lips again. "Nope, it's not the jam. It's the essence of you."

She gave a light tug on his hair. "Are you going

to kiss me for real, or are you planning to put me back to sleep?"

"You talked me into it." Lifting his hands, he captured her face and took command of her lips. His tongue claimed the inside of her mouth.

Heat seared Becca, leaving her weak, needy. She clung to Seth, arching into him, thrilling to the hard pressure of his erection against her belly.

"Oh, I need you." Grabbing a corner of the rumpled covers, he tossed them all the way down to the bottom of the bed. Then, he swept her down to lie gently on the mattress. "I need you now."

"Yes…please."

Standing by the bed in a pool of moonlight, Seth pulled the string of his pajama bottoms. They slid over his hips and down his long muscular legs. The sight of him, in full arousal, stole her breath. Stepping out of the pants, he slid onto the bed and between the thighs she parted in anticipation for him.

He lay there, staring into her face, allowing her to see the passionate need eating at him. His erection just touching the apex of her thighs, he braced his forearms on the mattress on either side of her head and crushed her mouth with his own.

Becca kissed him back with everything in her— her love, her need, everything. She dueled with his tongue, scraping her nails over his shoulders and down his back, thrilling to his grunt of pleasure.

Raising his body up onto his hands, Seth lowered his head to her breasts, laving the tips with his tongue before suckling first one then the other, driving her to the very edge of completion. She cried aloud in protest when he lifted his head to smile at her.

"Seth…" There was a note of pleading in her passion-roughened voice.

"Just one more kiss," he murmured, lowering his mouth to hers.

Becca parted her lips for his kiss and gasped with pleasure as he thrust his body into hers as he thrust his tongue into her mouth.

Curling her legs around his waist, Becca hung on to him, arching into the rhythm he set. Her breathing grew steadily harsher as tension spiraled tighter and tighter inside her.

When Becca was sure she couldn't take any more, the tension snapped, flinging her over the edge of reason. She cried out with the intensity of pleasure. A moment later, Seth's cry echoed her own.

When he rolled to the mattress beside her, she curled close to him, snuggling into his warmth. The air in the room was even chillier than before. She shivered.

Still, she protested when he disentangled himself from her, saying, "I'm cold."

"I know." Laughter tinged his voice. "I'm about

to take care of that." Sitting up, he pulled the covers up and over them, not neatly but effectively.

Becca murmured her appreciation in a near purr as he drew her to him, tucking the covers around them both. She was sound asleep within minutes.

Seth lay holding Becca in his arms, satiated—for the moment. A smile played across his lips. He had thought he was past the age to get hard again so soon after experiencing such a mind-bending orgasm.

Apparently not. His smile vanished and a very vulnerable part of his body jerked as Becca—still sleeping—slid one leg over his, her thigh resting against his hardening erection.

Damn, he thought. While it felt good, it was also a form of delicious torture. What to do. Without conscious direction, he moved his hand to stroke her thigh. He was further torturing himself with the feel of her soft skin against the hardest part of him.

Seth froze when Becca murmured and snuggled closer, when he didn't think it was possible for her to get any closer. Now her breast was pressing against his chest. He felt the sensation throughout his entire body. Oh, hell. He didn't want to wake her, while at the same time, he feared he'd burst if he didn't wake her.

What to do?

"Seth?"

Her soft voice was like balm to his body and soul. "I'm awake." In every particle of his body, he thought, suppressing a tremor.

"I…uh…" She hesitated and shifted around, damn near drawing a groan from him.

"What is it?" he asked, managing to sound reasonably calm, when he was anything but. "Bathroom?" he added when she shifted again. He silently sighed.

"No."

He could feel her shake her head. He swallowed, feeling her slide her leg back and forth against that most tender of spots. "More?" He hoped.

"Yesss," she said drawing the word out in tones of satisfaction for his understanding.

Seth began to caress her, make love to her. To his vast relief, Becca would have none of it. Grasping his hips, she pulled him over her, right between her legs.

"I don't want to wait, Seth," she said, kissing the corner of his mouth. "Next time…maybe."

That was encouraging, he thought. He was happy to oblige her every whim. Still, he took time to thoroughly kiss her senseless.

Unbelievably, it was even better than the first time. Seth fell asleep a very contented man.

It was barely light when Becca woke the second time. This time she did need the bathroom. Next to her, one arm circling her waist, Seth was softly snoring. Smiling, she carefully moved his arm and slid away and over the side of the bed.

Shivering in the chill air, she answered nature's call, made fast work of a washup, and quickly brushed her teeth. Practically running, she made a beeline back to the bed, slipping beneath the covers to snuggle close to Seth again.

To her disappointment, he slid out of the bed on the other side. "My turn," he said, flashing a grin at her before striding into the bathroom. Five minutes later, he got back into the bed and snuggled up next to her.

"Damn cold out there," he muttered, drawing her tightly against him.

"I know," Becca agreed, catching the smell of her soap on his skin and the minty scent of her toothpaste on his breath. "Warm in here though."

"Yeah." He smoothed a hand down the side of her body. "Were you thinking of going back to sleep?"

"Eventually," she said, gliding her palm down his chest, smiling when he sucked in a breath. "Did you have something else in mind?"

"Well—" he began.

"Would you like to discuss the world situation?" she interrupted to ask, managing a straight face and somber tone. "The economy?"

Thrilling her with his bark of laughter, Seth rolled on top of her. "Oh, I think we can come up with something much more interesting than that." His smile was blatantly sexy. "And I do mean come up with."

Feeling wonderfully wanton, Becca slid her hand farther down his torso to curl around the hard length of him. "I see…er, feel what you mean."

Seth was laughing when he kissed her; his laughter quickly ceased, his kiss becoming gentle, coaxing, luring her into participation…as if she needed any coaxing or luring.

This time, he made slow, exquisite love to her, arousing not only her body but her emotions as well.

Murmuring his appreciation of her complete acceptance of him, Seth turned her on her side, away from him, and curled up behind her, spoon fashion. Becca sighed as he stroked her body, and drifted into a deep sleep.

It was near noon when Becca woke once more. Bright autumn sunlight streamed through the bedroom windows. Next to her, Seth yawned and stretched.

"Time to get up already?" he asked, running his fingers through his hair.

"Already?" Becca said, laughing. "It's nearly lunchtime."

"Humph," he mumbled, "that must be why I'm feeling half-starved."

Shaking her head, Becca tossed back the covers. She shivered and Seth yelped at the touch of chilly air against his bare skin. He reached for the comforter. Taking it with her, she jumped from the bed.

"I'm going to shower." She laughed again at his pained expression. "I suggest you do the same."

"What if I want to go back to sleep?" he called after her as she stepped into the bathroom.

"Do it in your own bed upstairs," she called back. "I'm going to pull the sheets again after I shower and dress."

"You changed the sheets just yesterday," he shouted as she shut the door.

"And I'm changing them today," she shouted back. "So take a hike upstairs." Grinning, she turned the water on for the shower full-force. She started as the door was suddenly pushed open and Seth stuck his head inside.

"Why can't I shower with you?" He gave her a dangerously sexy smile.

Becca didn't bother to answer, simply because she felt he wouldn't take a refusal anyway. "Seth, get out of my bathroom," she ordered. "I'm freezing and I want a hot shower. Get your own shower. Oh, and on your way upstairs, turn the thermostat up on the heater."

Heaving a heavy sigh, he pulled his head back and shut the door. But even over the sound of the shower spray she heard him call, "You don't know what you're missing, Becca."

"You mean it gets better?" she yelled to be heard, nearly choking on a burst of laughter.

"Oh, do I have 'better' waiting for you," he yelled back, laughter in his voice. The door shut with a telling bang.

Becca was still smiling when she stepped from the shower. Her smile fled as the still cold air brushed her naked body and dripping wet hair. Wrapping one towel around her head, she grabbed another to dry her shivering body. Dry, she tossed the damp towel in the hamper and hurried into the bedroom to dress and blow-dry her hair.

By the time she had stripped the sheets from the bed and remade it, Becca could feel warm air wafting from the vents in the floor.

Dressed in jeans, a cotton knit pullover sweater and her fuzzy slippers, Becca left the bedroom, tugging the rolling hamper behind her. She went directly to the laundry room to dump the sheets into the washer before heading to the kitchen.

"What kept you?" Seth said as she entered the room. "I was about to eat without you."

Becca raised her eyebrows at the sight of him. She wasn't surprised to see he had fixed the coffee, as she had smelled it the moment she'd left her room. But she was surprised to see he had also fixed breakfast. Without a word, she observed his handiwork. Seth simply stood there, looking casual yet terrific in snug-fitting jeans and a dark-brown sweatshirt, a smile on his face as he watched her.

Ignoring the little flutter inside at the mere look of him, she shifted her gaze to his domestic handiwork.

There were strips of fried bacon draining on a paper-towel-covered plate. She caught the scent of cinnamon coming from the four slices of French toast cooking in a large frying pan.

The table was set for two, large glasses of water and small glasses of orange juice set at each place. She watched, bemused, as he turned to neatly flip the bread over in the pan.

"Do you cook often?" she asked, dryly. "Or is French toast and bacon your limit?"

"I've been a bachelor for a long time," he said, just as dryly. "It was either learn to cook for myself, eat frozen dinners, or in restaurants every day. I decided to learn to cook." He lifted a piece of the toast with a spatula. "Perfect, I'll dish up. You can pour the coffee."

Hungry, and tingling from his attention, Becca was happy to comply.

"Hmm, delicious," she murmured with her first bite of toast. "Did your mother teach you to cook?" It seemed a natural assumption, as Becca's mother had taught her at an early age.

"Good grief, no." Seth laughed. "My mother is a lousy cook. Fortunately, my father can afford to pay for an excellent cook. I learned, trial and error, from a number of cookbooks."

Becca laughed with him, then grew quiet as she devoured every morsel he had served her. After lingering over second cups of coffee, they made short shrift of cleaning up the kitchen.

"Is there someplace I can get a newspaper around here?" Seth asked as Becca started for the laundry room to switch loads.

"Yes." She flashed a grin at him. "At the end of the driveway there's a mailbox. The paper will be in it." She stopped him as he headed for the door. "If you want to wait till I put on shoes, I'll walk along with you and get some fresh air."

"I was gonna take the car." A smile teased his lips and his eyes.

Becca merely gave him a look. His smiled graduated into a laugh.

"Okay, we'll walk."

"Damn straight," she muttered, chuckling as she bypassed the laundry room to walk to the bedroom. Along with her shoes, Becca took a lightweight jacket from the closet, just in case.

It was a cool but beautiful late September day, sunlight sparkling off myriad colors of the changing leaves of the deciduous trees on the mountains.

At the mailbox, Seth collected the paper and arched a brow at her. "How about a walk before we go back inside?"

"Okay," Becca agreed, slipping the jacket over her shoulders. "Which direction?"

"Let's just follow one of those side paths we passed on our way down," he suggested. "See where they lead, if anywhere."

"Fine." She turned, heading back up the drive, and started as, falling into step beside her, Seth curled his long-fingered hand around hers.

Controlling her breathing pattern with effort, she strolled along, as if walking hand in hand with him was an everyday occurrence. Her pulse leapt when he laced his fingers through hers.

They talked as they strolled, following where the path led them. They discussed the nice weather, the beautiful mountains, the town below, but not at any time did the conversation flow into their personal lives. Not one word was mentioned about their work, or the agreement they had struck to spend the next five days of his vacation together both in and out of bed.

They laughed at the realization that the path had meandered around in a wide circle, ending at the house, near where it had begun.

Becca, aching inside, smiling outside, loved the

sound of Seth's laughter, loved laughing with him…loved him more than she cared to acknowledge.

But, there it was, glowing like a light inside her. She loved him unconditionally, with every cell and atom in her mind and body.

And yet, as much as she was enjoying every minute of being with him, Becca had come to a hard-made decision. When Seth left at the end of that week, it would be the last she would see him.

The very idea of never seeing him again hurt badly, but loving him as she did, Becca knew she could not keep going in the role of his mistress, nor could she work so closely with him as his assistant under those circumstances. When Seth left on Saturday, he would unknowingly be taking her heart and love with him.

On the other hand, when she left the cabin, and she knew it would be soon, she would not be returning to Philadelphia, possibly not even Pennsylvania.

As they neared the house, Becca vowed to herself to live to the fullest, savor ever minute of these few remaining days with him. She was certain they would have to last her the rest of her life, for she could not foresee any other man ever taking his place in her heart.

"You've grown very quiet," Seth said as they mounted the stairs to the porch. "Something wrong?"

"No." Becca shook her head, and worked up a smile and an excuse for her silence. "I noticed that Sue's car isn't here, so I've been thinking about what to make for dinner later."

He came to an abrupt stop at the door, a frown drawing his dark brows together. "Do you think they might have had an emergency at the clinic?"

"Oh, I never thought of that," she said, rushing into the house and straight to the phone. "I'll call down there and..."

"Wait a minute," Seth said, bringing her up short with her hand on the phone's receiver. "Sue must have been here while we were out." He held up a piece of paper. "There's a note on the table from her."

"Read it, please," she said, walking back to the table as he read aloud.

"'Becca and Seth...although I may be wrong, I doubt it.'" Seth glanced up from the note to grin at her before reading on. "'But I believe you two have a thing going on, the same as John and I have. So, I've decided to give all four of us a break. John and I will be staying at my house until Saturday. Becca, you won't need to come in to the clinic this week, either, as I will be working there with John all week. Have fun, Sue.'"

Seth glanced up at her when he'd finished, his

eyes bright with laughter. "How thoughtful of Sue," he said, laughing aloud.

"Hmm," Becca murmured, nodding in agreement. "But whatever will we do with all that time together?" she mused aloud, her lips quivering with laughter.

"Well, right now, you are going to go toss the sheets into the dryer."

The look Becca gave him clearly indicated she couldn't believe he'd said that. "I see." Of course, she didn't, and said so. "And what will you be doing while I busy myself with the laundry?"

"I'm going to turn down the thermostat," he answered, in apparent seriousness.

She frowned in confusion. "Why?"

"Because I'm going to build a fire." He pulled a broad, laughable leer. "After that, I'm going to spread the furry throw on the floor in front of it."

Warmth and excitement begun to bloom inside Becca. As if puzzled, she fluttered her eyelashes as she repeated in all innocence, "Why?"

He wiggled his eyebrows suggestively. "So we can have an orgy. Or twelve."

Becca, suppressing a shiver of expectation, leered right back at him. "Or even a dozen."

Laughing again, he circled the table to take her in his arms. "You are something else," he said, kissing her soundly. Turning her away, he gave her a light nudge toward the laundry room. He strode into the living room, calling back, "It won't take be long to start a fire, so get it in gear. I'm aiming for a full baker's dozen." He turned to flash a smile at her.

"No kidding," she said, flashing one right back at him. "I can't wait."

Ten

It was late Saturday morning, Becca stood next to Seth beside his car. His bag was in the trunk, the driver's-side door was open. Soon he would slide behind the wheel and drive away, out of her life.

Since Monday, the days had flown by. Becca, determined to stick to her agreement to spend the remainder of the week with him, had put everything from her mind but Seth. They cooked, took walks, talked and laughed, made near desperate love at the merest suggestion…and there were many.

She wanted to cry. She wanted to grab ahold of him and beg him not to go. She did neither of those things. Instead, she schooled her expression into one of calm composure. There would be plenty of time for crying later after he was gone.

After she was alone.

"I wish you'd come home with me, Becca," Seth said, chasing away her troubling thoughts. "Your physical condition is back to normal." A wisp of a smile touched his lips. "That's obvious from the way you kept up…with our long walks, and other exercise."

"I'm not ready to go back yet," she said, thinking she very likely never would be.

"I know you're not ready to go back to work," he said. "I could tell that from the way you reacted after we were finished treating that boy. Emotionally, you appeared ready to pass out."

"I know." She managed a smile.

"I need you beside me…" His voice was rough, a little strained. "I need you beside me in my bed, and in the operating room."

If he had left it at the first part, Becca might have given in, surrendered to her own need to be with him. But she wanted more, she wanted to be with him in every way, not just as his bed partner and operating-room assistant.

"I'm not ready, Seth," she repeated, her throat thickening and her eyes stinging with tears, longing for him to stay, wishing he would go.

"Okay." Stepping to her, Seth drew her into his

arms, crushing her to him, his mouth to hers. He reluctantly released her. "Take as much time as you need, and keep in touch to let me know how you're feeling."

She made do with a nod. "Goodbye, Seth. I'll…miss you. Drive safely."

"I always do." He smiled and slid behind the wheel. "I'll miss you, too." Holding her gaze for long seconds, he started the car, waved and drove away.

Tears rolling down her face, Becca watched his car until it disappeared around the curve at the end of the driveway.

He should have told her he loved her.

The thought tormented Seth all the way back to Philadelphia. *Why hadn't he?* That thought always followed the first one. Of course, he knew the answer. Fear of her rejection kept him silent.

Becca had never given him the slightest hint she felt anything for him but respect for his expertise as a physician and surgeon. His lips twisted in a bitter smile. Oh, she had obviously appreciated his expertise in bed. She had been as eager for his body as he had for hers.

She had admitted she had been a long time without a man, and he was certain she had not been with a man the entire time she had spent in Africa. So her physical response to him was normal and understandable.

Becca had given him no indication whatsoever love had anything to do with their time together.

Seth sighed. Even so, he longed for her to come home.

Should she have confessed, told Seth she loved him—had loved him almost since first joining his surgical team? Becca had lost count of the times she had asked herself that question. The answer that sprang to mind was always the same. Had she told him, even hinted at her feelings for him, in all probability she would have been standing in the driveway, choking on his dust as he drove hell for leather away from her.

Seth was in his thirties; apparently he didn't want to get seriously involved with any woman. Sex, even fantastic sex, was one thing. Obviously love didn't factor into his life, his work.

Becca didn't keep in contact with Seth. He tried to reach her, but she didn't answer either his calls or e-mails. What could she say to him? She knew that soon she'd have to tell him she had no intention of going back to Philadelphia, or possibly even Pennsylvania. But she kept putting it off till later.

By the end of the second week after Seth had left, Becca was certain she was pregnant. All the signs were there. Not only had she missed her period, her breasts were tender and felt a bit larger, and she was tired and sleepy most of the time.

It was time to leave the cabin. Sue, having come back to stay at the house with Becca after Seth departed, fussed over her, but at least she didn't pry into why Becca wouldn't take his calls.

Becca didn't hesitate. She told Sue she was leaving that same evening over dinner. "I've loafed around long enough," she said when Sue protested. "It's time I got back into the swing."

"You're going back to work with Seth?" Sue asked, a hopeful note in her voice.

"First, I'm going to visit my parents in Virginia," she said, avoiding a direct answer. "Afterward, maybe I'll drive to Atlanta to see my sister. I'm going to call the number given to me and thank whoever answers for the use of this lovely house, but I'm going to pass on the limo. Is there anywhere I can rent a car?"

"Yes, in the city," Sue said, smiling. "Where the hospital is located. And you're in luck. I was planning to drive into the mall there later this week." Her smile softened. "John's birthday is next week and I want to get him something special. You can go with me if next week is okay for you."

"That's fine, I'm really not in a hurry," Becca said, thinking a few days wouldn't make any difference.

"After you leave, I'll close the house," Sue went on. "As I'll be working full-time with John, I'm not going to be available to be the standby housekeeper anymore."

Four days later, Becca stood hugging Sue in the parking lot of the car rental firm. Her luggage was already stowed in the trunk of the late-model compact she had rented.

"I'm going to miss you, Becca," Sue said, sniffing as she stepped back. "So is John."

"I'm going to miss you and John, too." Becca swiped a hand over her moist eyes. "You've spoiled me rotten over the past two months."

"It's been fun." Sue's smile was watery. "Hard to believe it's late autumn already." She glanced around her. "The leaves are falling and before you know it, it'll be Christmas." Saying the word seemed to perk her up. "Hey, as long as I'm shopping for a birthday present, I might as well look for a Christmas present for John."

"Then you'd better get at it." Becca laughed. "And I'd better get moving if I hope to arrive at my parents' house before dark." One more hug, and Becca got into the car and drove away.

The test was positive, as Becca was certain it would be. It was only then, in the bathroom of her parents' lovely home, that the full impact of it hit her. She was pregnant. A part of her and Seth was already forming inside her body. Her baby.

Seth's baby.

The thought brought her up short. Seth's baby. He didn't have to know. In all probability, he wouldn't want to know, she rationalized.

Becca had saved her money since her first job at sixteen, when she had worked part-time in one of the shops not far from her home in Philadelphia. She had a very healthy bank balance, more than enough to last her until the baby was born, and for some time after. With her credentials, she could find a job almost anywhere, in any number of hospitals or doctors' offices in Pennsylvania.

The idea wasn't at all scary.

Becca spent a week with her parents. She played a round of golf with her father. She went shopping with her mother. And the three of them enjoyed a lovely day in Colonial Williamsburg, always a thrill for Becca as she was an American history buff.

She had to forego her visit to Rachael. Her parents told Becca that her sister was on a business trip to San Francisco.

When the week was over, Becca started back for Philadelphia, using the long trip to plan for her eventual move from the city. There would be so much to do—look for another location, then a job, after that a place to live, sublet her apartment, pack and arrange for shipping her furniture.

It made her tired simply thinking about it.

The Philadelphia area was enjoying mild late October weather. Lugging her cases from the car to her apartment, Becca felt too warm in the turtleneck sweater she had pulled on that morning.

Inside her apartment, she dumped the bags, leaned back against the door and sighed. It felt good to be home. "We're home, baby," she whispered, splaying her hand protectively over her belly.

Pushing away from the door, she made a quick glance around the place, satisfied with the job done by the lady that cleaned for her once a week. The place was dust-free and smelled fresh.

After the long hours of driving, with stops only to grab a bite to eat, Becca was tired. Picking up the cases once more, she carried them into her bedroom and let them drop again. The next moment she herself dropped, onto the neatly made bed.

Expecting to have a nap, she closed her eyes, but sleep eluded her. Several thoughts she had determinedly ignored for several days finally broke through her mental barrier.

First and foremost was the acknowledgment that she had to tell Seth she was pregnant. As the father of the baby, he had a right to know. Not once did she so much as consider the idea that he might deny responsibility, or at least his part in it.

Secondly, she admitted to herself that she didn't

want to relocate. She wanted to remain in Philadelphia, and she wanted to work at the University of Pennsylvania Hospital, if not with Seth, then as a floor nurse. She didn't want to—*couldn't*—work with another surgeon.

Knowing what she had to do, Becca heaved a sigh of defeat, pushed herself up to sit on the edge of the bed and reached for the phone on the nightstand.

Seth's private secretary, Judy Miller, answered on the second ring. "Hi, Judy, it's Becca Jameson," she said. "Is Dr. Andrews available?"

"Oh, hi, Becca, how are you?"

"I'm fine, good as new," Becca answered, injecting a jaunty note into her voice. "I need to talk to Seth."

"I'm sorry but he's not here. He cleared his calendar for today and Monday. May I leave him a message?"

"Yes, please, Judy. Tell him I'd like to talk to him at his convenience."

Feeling deflated, Becca sat for a long time.

Knowing she'd now not be able to nap, she got up and began unpacking her bags. Later, she would make a run to the supermarket to restock her fridge. After that, she'd do her laundry, then find other things to do, every day until Seth called her.

Her telephone didn't ring the entire weekend or

for most of Monday. But her doorbell rang late Monday afternoon. The ring was immediately followed by a sharp rap on the door.

Knowing who was on the other side of the door, Becca drew a deep breath, wet her suddenly dry lips and went to the door to open it.

"Where in hell have you been?" Seth demanded, storming past her into the room.

"I was visiting my parents," she answered as calmly as she could.

"Yeah, for one week." He looked about to explode. "Dammit, Becca, I know up until you left for Virginia you were at the cabin. Why didn't you answer my calls or e-mails? I was going nuts worrying about you."

Oh, the doctor was back on duty, she thought. "I…er, needed some time to myself. Why were you worried? You knew where I was," she said.

He exhaled, as if to let off steam. "Becca, you didn't answer my phone calls, you didn't respond to my e-mails. I didn't know what to think. Hell, you could have died for all I knew."

"But—"

"I'm not finished," he interrupted, on a roll. "Friday, I drove down there, only to find the cabin dark and deserted. So, I went to the clinic. Sue told me where you'd gone and that you were fine. I got back to my apartment not half an hour ago, to find a message from Judy on my voice mail, telling me you had called me Friday."

"Yes, I did." Becca was having difficulty maintaining her composure. His rant was beginning to unnerve her.

"Why?" he nearly yelled at her.

"Why, what?" She was starting to tremble at the idea of telling him about her condition when he was obviously so very angry.

"First off, why didn't you answer my calls or e-mails?"

"Because I didn't want to talk to you." Now she was getting angry. Who did he think he was, yelling at her? "And before you can ask, I'll tell you why. I didn't want you to know I wasn't planning on staying here, or working here with you anymore."

His eyes narrowed. "Why not? After the week we spent together…" His softened voice was almost scarier than his shouting.

"Because I had no intention of being your assistant in the operating room during the day, and your bedmate at night."

"You certainly made no objections about being my bedmate at the cabin." Seth's voice was harsh. "In fact, you appeared to revel in it."

"That was before I knew the reveling would make me pregnant," she shouted at him.

"I made you pregnant?"

He was clearly astonished, which made her madder. "Yes, you did it! Who else?" she retorted, getting angrier by the second.

"And so you were simply going to take off for parts unknown," he snapped back at her. "Is that it?"

Becca angled her chin defiantly at him. "Yes, I was planning to take off."

In a blink he went absolutely statue-still. His features went rock-hard. His eyes were like amber chips in ice. "You were thinking about an abortion?"

As if he had struck her, Becca recoiled, but recovered quickly. "No! Never! This is my baby. You have nothing to say about it."

Within two long strides he was standing inches in front of her. "I have plenty to say about it, dammit!" His voice was tough, adamant. "If you're pregnant, I'm pregnant, too."

Stunned by his flat authoritative statement, she stared at him, speechless. Seth took advantage of her momentary silence and, fortunately, in a more reasonable tone of voice.

"I'm relieved to hear you weren't considering abortion, Becca. The idea of you wanting to get rid of my baby sickened me."

"I never gave it a thought, Seth." Suddenly, Becca was exhausted, physically and emotionally. "I wasn't going to tell you. I was just thinking of relocating and taking care of the baby myself."

He closed his eyes and an expression of pain flickered across his face. "Oh, Becca…"

"I'm sorry for ever thinking you wouldn't care." Her voice held a soft sadness. "I realized Friday that you had the right to know, and I had to tell you. That's why I called your office."

"You believed I wouldn't want my baby, our baby?" He placed a palm on her still flat belly. "Of course I want it. I love the baby already, almost as much as I want and love you."

"Wh-what?" she could barely whisper.

He cradled her face in his hands. "Becca, I love you, I have been in love with you for what seems like forever."

"But…you never said…" Tears filled her eyes. "You never…I thought…"

"That I just wanted sex, your body?" Seth's smile was heartbreaking.

"Yes." Becca met his gaze steadily, bravely.

"I did." He kissed her. "I do." He kissed her again. "But I want more, I want all of you, you heart, your mind, your soul." His smile now teased. "Your body and the fantastic sex we have together."

"Oh, Seth," she murmured, sighing.

"And if you don't soon tell me you love me, too," he said in warning, "I'm going to have a freaking nervous breakdown right here."

"I love you, Dr. Seth Andrews," Becca confessed, nearly choking on rising laughter. "We've been such idiots all this time, we deserve each other."

Although he was laughing with her, both their laughter was silenced when his mouth took hers.

Becca and Seth were married at her parents' home the day after Thanksgiving. Seth stole her breath away, looking so handsome in a dark suit and white silk shirt. He claimed she stole his breath in the plain midcalf-length, high-necked, long-sleeved white velvet wedding dress. They left Virginia the day after the wedding, to honeymoon in a place known only to them.

They arrived at their destination in late afternoon. It was unfamiliar to Becca, though it was very familiar to Seth. It should have been. The honeymoon site was the condo Seth had bought and lived in for years.

Perfect. They didn't leave the apartment or answer the phones, cell or landline. Other than switching the cooking of meals every other day, they rarely left the bed. Perfect indeed.

When Becca and Seth returned to her apartment to begin packing her things to be moved to his place, she found an intriguing-looking envelope among her weeklong pile of mail. It contained an invitation that was both terse and formal. It read:

The honor of your presence is required at an undisclosed location, December twenty-fourth of this year, at eight o'clock in the evening, for a black-tie affair, at which time an explanation concerning your recent anonymous gift will be offered.

Enclosed are the pertinent travel arrangements for both you and one guest of your choosing.

That was it. No signature. The travel arrangements listed a limousine to collect her and guest at her apartment, which meant the location was in or around Philadelphia.

Becca read the invitation aloud to Seth. When she finished, she glanced up at him, frowning. "What do you think?"

"Sounds intriguing, I think we should go," he said, using the excuse of scanning the invitation again to come to stand behind her, coil his arms around her waist, press close to her and read over her shoulder. "What do you think?"

"From the feel of something back there," she drawled, "I think we should go to bed."

He laughed, turned her around, drew her into his arms and soundly kissed her. "I think that's a great idea. But, do you want to go to the gala?"

"Oh, that, yes, let's go. If not fun it should at least prove interesting."

"Okay, but you must wear your wedding dress."

Becca smiled. "Okay, if you insist, but why?"

"Because your tummy is still flat, and you looked so beautiful in it."

Her smile softened. "I knew there was a reason I loved you," she whispered, giving him a quick kiss. "I'll wear the dress on one condition."

"Fine. Name it."

"We go shopping for something to relieve the stark white." Her eyes brightened. "I know, something festive, a pin maybe…no, a sash in silver, red and green."

"Anything you want." Seth swept her up in his arms. "But first we make use of the bed, then we go shopping."

Wrapping her arms around his neck, Becca sighed in delicious contentment.

* * * * *

One

There were no half-naked nymphets scattering flower petals and the red Porsche wasn't exactly a classic chariot, but the man getting out of it was a certified Greek God. Emily Raines rested her forearms on the handle of the still unplugged industrial floor sander and watched the stranger through the front window. Tall, broad shoulders, narrow hips and dark hair just long enough to blow in the light breeze. The easy way he moved as he reached back inside the car for his suit jacket…

"Emily!"

Half her brain recognized her friend's arrival from somewhere in the old building. The other half went on with a fantasy of see-through togas, reclining sofas and grapes.

Okay, he was crossing the street. "It looks like we're going to have a visitor."

Her friend Beth glanced toward the glass front doors and grinned. "Scream if you need help," she offered, laughing and heading for the door at the back of the office. "Loud if you're serious about it. It's a big building."

Need help? Ha! Emily glanced back toward the front just long enough to gauge her timing, and then began to ever-so-casually unwind the cord of the sander. The bell over the door jangled. Emily put what she hoped looked like a serene-but-pleasantly-semisurprised smile on her face and looked up.

"Hello," Adonis said.

Oh, be still her heart. A voice that rumbled, deep and slow and low.

"Hi," she vaguely heard herself reply as she watched his gaze slide slowly down to openly marvel over the fact that she'd bought her T-shirt in Jackson Hole. It moved lower still to the frayed edges of her cutoff jeans and right on down, smooth as silk, to the tops of her leather work boots. It returned upward—every bit as appreciatively—to finally meet her own.

He smiled, lopsidedly, the light in his eyes a delicious combination of guilt and pleasure.

Emily reined in her own smile and managed to tamp the more obvious notes of hope out of her voice as she asked, "What can I do for you?"

The guilt part evaporated out of his smile and his eyes sparkled with clear understanding. "I'm Cole Preston and I'm wondering if you've seen my grandmother this morning. She said she was coming here. Ida Bentley?"

Well, this was even better. Hardly a stranger at all. Emily grinned. "Ida's an absolute sweetheart. A truly incredible woman."

Sadness replaced the easy pleasure in his smile as he nodded. "She's also got a few screws that aren't quite as tight as they used to be. And I have the checkbook to prove it."

"Well, yes," Emily allowed diplomatically as her stomach fluttered and went a little cold. "I have noticed that Ida's mind tends to drift a bit every now and then."

"More than a bit," he countered. "And every now and then is more like often."

So much for the hope of Mr. Wonderful wandering in off the street. The man certainly looked like the stuff of feminine dreams, but the nice suit and the well-honed body only disguised the fact that he had all the emotional sensitivity of...of...well, she'd think of something really cold and heartless later.

At the moment, all she could really think about

was how pathetically desperate she was. To think she'd been willing to drop her toga and share her grapes with him… Shaking her head and silently mourning the untimely—and not to mention brutally quick—death of the most inspiring fantasy she'd had in years, Emily plugged the cord of the sander into the wall socket.

"I haven't seen Ida this morning, Mr. Preston. She could be over at the café or the gift shop. You might check there."

"Well, maybe it's a good thing she isn't here yet," he said, either missing the fact that he'd been dismissed, or choosing to ignore it. Neither possibility counted in his favor. "It'll give me a chance to take care of business."

Business? She wasn't a business. She was a nonprofit community organization for the elderly. Or would be once she got the place fixed up. Not that she needed to tell him any of that. Holding the handles of the floor sander in the classic I'm-busy-let's-get-this-over-with pose, she met his gaze again. Or tried to, anyway. His gaze was taking another fantastic voyage to her boot laces and back. Since his attention was otherwise engaged…

Emily considered the long length of his lean legs, the broad width of his chest, the way the dark hair at his nape brushed against the crisp white of his shirt collar. She arched a brow.

Maybe she'd been too quick to give up the torrid-affair thing. It wasn't as though she was looking for Prince Charming and the whole forever-in-a-happy-castle deal. Cole Preston was sculpted, hot, and no doubt about it, interested. It would be a real shame to waste such an incredible opportunity.

And not just a shame, either. It could very well be a crime. Like leaving a perfectly fitting pair of jeans in the store dressing room was a crime against the shopping gods. Wonderful things were put in your path for a reason and you took a big chance if you didn't properly appreciate them. And, gosh, she certainly didn't want to risk offending the gods of a breathless good time.

* * * * *

Turn the page for a sneak preview of
AFTERSHOCK,
a new anthology featuring
New York Times *bestselling author*
Sharon Sala.

Available October 2008.

n✸cturne™

Dramatic and sensual tales
of paranormal romance.

Chapter 1

October
New York City

Nicole Masters was sitting cross-legged on her sofa while a cold autumn rain peppered the windows of her fourth-floor apartment. She was poking at the ice cream in her bowl and trying not to be in a mood.

Six weeks ago, a simple trip to her neighborhood pharmacy had turned into a nightmare. She'd walked into the middle of a robbery. She never even saw the man who shot her in the head and left her for dead. She'd survived, but some of her senses had not. She was dealing with short-term memory loss and a tendency to stagger. Even though she'd been told the problems were most likely temporary, she waged a daily battle with depression.

Her parents had been killed in a car wreck when she was twenty-one. And except for a few friends—and most recently her boyfriend, Dominic Tucci, who lived in the apartment right above hers—she was alone. Her doctor kept reminding her that she should be grateful to be alive, and on one level she knew he was right. But he wasn't living in her shoes.

If she'd been anywhere else but at that pharmacy when the robbery happened, she wouldn't have died twice on the way to the hospital. Instead of being grateful that she'd survived, she couldn't stop thinking of what she'd lost.

But that wasn't the end of her troubles. On top of everything else, something strange was happening inside her head. She'd begun to hear odd things: sounds, not voices—at least, she didn't think it was voices. It was more like the distant noise of rapids—a rush of wind and water inside her head that, when it came, blocked out everything around her. It didn't happen often, but when it did, it was frightening, and it was driving her crazy.

The blank moments, which is what she called them, even had a rhythm. First there came that sound, then a cold sweat, then panic with no reason.

Part of her feared it was the beginning of an emotional breakdown. And part of her feared it wasn't—that it was going to turn out to be a permanent souvenir of her resurrection.

Frustrated with herself and the situation as it stood, she upped the sound on the TV remote. But instead of *Wheel of Fortune,* an announcer broke in with a special bulletin.

"This just in. Police are on the scene of a kidnapping that occurred only hours ago at The Dakota. Molly Dane, the six-year-old daughter of one of Hollywood's blockbuster stars, Lyla Dane, was taken by force from the family apartment. At this time they have yet to receive a ransom demand. The housekeeper was seriously injured during the abduction, and is, at the present time, in surgery. Police are hoping to be able to talk to her once she regains consciousness. In the meantime, we are going now to a press conference with Lyla Dane."

Horrified, Nicole stilled as the cameras went live to where the actress was speaking before a bank of microphones. The shock and terror in Lyla Dane's voice were physically painful to watch. But even though Nicole kept upping the volume, the sound continued to fade.

Just when she was beginning to think something was wrong with her set, the broadcast suddenly switched from the Dane press conference to what appeared to be footage of the kidnapping, beginning with footage from inside the apartment.

When the front door suddenly flew back against the wall and four men rushed in, Nicole gasped. Horrified, she quickly realized that this must have been caught on a security camera inside the Dane apartment.

As Nicole continued to watch, a small Asian woman, who she guessed was the maid, rushed forward in an effort to keep them out. When one of the men hit her in the face with his gun, Nicole moaned. The violence was too reminiscent of what she'd lived through. Sick to her stomach, she fisted her hands against her belly, wishing it was over, but unable to tear her gaze away.

When the maid dropped to the carpet, the same man followed with a vicious kick to the little woman's midsection that lifted her off the floor.

"Oh, my God," Nicole said. When blood began to pool beneath the maid's head, she started to cry.

As the tape played on, the four men split up in different directions. The camera caught one running down a long marble hallway, then disappearing into a room. Moments later he reappeared, carrying a little girl, who Nicole assumed was Molly Dane. The child was wearing a pair of red pants and a white turtleneck sweater, and her hair was partially blocking her abductor's face as he carried her down the hall. She was kicking and screaming in his arms, and when he slapped her, it elicited an agonized scream that brought the other three running. Nicole watched in horror as one of them ran up and put his hand over Molly's face. Seconds later, she went limp.

One moment they were in the foyer, then they were gone.

Nicole jumped to her feet, then staggered drunkenly. The bowl of ice cream she'd absentmindedly placed in her lap shattered at her feet, splattering glass and melting ice cream everywhere.

The picture on the screen abruptly switched from the kidnapping to what Nicole assumed was a rerun of Lyla Dane's plea for her daughter's safe return, but she was numb.

Before she could think what to do next, the doorbell rang. Startled by the unexpected sound, she shakily swiped at the tears and took a step forward. She didn't feel the glass shards piercing her feet until she took the second step. At that point, sharp pains shot through her foot. She gasped, then looked down in confusion. Her legs looked as if she'd been running through mud, and she was standing in broken glass and ice cream, while a thin ribbon of blood seeped out from beneath her toes.

"Oh, no," Nicole mumbled, then stifled a second moan of pain.

The doorbell rang again. She shivered, then clutched her head in confusion.

"Just a minute!" she yelled, then tried to sidestep the rest of the debris as she hobbled to the door.

When she looked through the peephole in the door, she didn't know whether to be relieved or regretful.

It was Dominic, and as usual, she was a mess.

Nicole smiled a little self-consciously as she opened the door to let him in. "I just don't know what's happening to me. I think I'm losing my mind."

"Hey, don't talk about my woman like that."

Nicole rode the surge of delight his words brought. "So I'm still your woman?"

Dominic lowered his head.

Their lips met.

The kiss proceeded.

Slowly.

Thoroughly.

* * * * *

Be sure to look for the
AFTERSHOCK *anthology next month,*
as well as other exciting paranormal stories
from Silhouette Nocturne.
Available in October wherever books are sold.

nocturne™

NEW YORK TIMES BESTSELLING AUTHOR

SHARON SALA

JANIS REAMES HUDSON
DEBRA COWAN

AFTERSHOCK

Three women are brought to the brink of death...
only to discover the aftershock of their trauma has
left them with unexpected and unwelcome gifts of
paranormal powers. Now each woman must learn to
accept her newfound abilities while fighting for life,
love and second chances....

Available October wherever books are sold.

www.eHarlequin.com
www.paranormalromanceblog.wordpress.com   SN61796

REQUEST YOUR FREE BOOKS!

2 FREE NOVELS PLUS 2 FREE GIFTS!

Silhouette Desire®

Passionate, Powerful, Provocative!

SDES08R

SPECIAL EDITION™

BRAVO FAMILY TIES

Tanner Bravo and Crystal Cerise had it bad
for each other, though they couldn't be more
different. Tanner was the type to settle down;
free-spirited Crystal wouldn't hear of it.
Now that Crystal was pregnant, would
Tanner have his way after all?

Look for

HAVING
TANNER BRAVO'S
BABY

by *USA TODAY* bestselling author
CHRISTINE RIMMER

Available in October wherever books are sold.

Romantic
SUSPENSE

Sparked by Danger, Fueled by Passion.

USA TODAY bestselling author

Merline Lovelace

Undercover Wife

Secret agent Mike Callahan, code name Hawkeye,
objects when he's paired with sophisticated
Gillian Ridgeway on a dangerous spy mission
to Hong Kong. Gillian has secretly been in love
with him for years, but Hawk is an overprotective
man with a wounded past that threatens to
resurface. Now the two must put their lives—
and hearts—at risk for each other.

Available October wherever books are sold.

COMING NEXT MONTH

#1897 MARRIAGE, MANHATTAN STYLE—Barbara Dunlop
Park Avenue Scandals
Secrets, blackmail and infertility had their marriage on the rocks.
Will an unexpected opportunity at parenthood give them a second
chance?

#1898 THE MONEY MAN'S SEDUCTION—Leslie LaFoy
Gifts from a Billionaire
Suspicious of her true motives, he vows to keep her close—but as
close as in his bed?

#1899 DANTE'S CONTRACT MARRIAGE—Day Leclaire
The Dante Legacy
Forced to marry to protect an infamous diamond, they never
counted on being struck by The Dante Inferno. Suddenly their
convenient marriage is full of *in*convenient passion.

#1900 AN AFFAIR WITH THE PRINCESS—Michelle Celmer
Royal Seductions
He'd had an affair with the princess, once upon a time. But why
had he returned? Remembrance…or revenge?

#1901 MISTAKEN MISTRESS—Tessa Radley
The Saxon Brides
Could this woman he feels such a reckless passion for really be
his late brother's mistress? Or are there other secrets she's hiding?

#1902 BABY BENEFITS—Emily McKay
Billionaires and Babies
Her boss had a baby—and he needed her help. How could she
possibly deny him…how could she ever resist him?

SDCNM0908